GOOD
ENOUGH
TO EAT

Published in the UK by Scholastic, 2022
1 London Bridge, London, SE1 9BA
Scholastic Ireland, 89E Lagan Road, Dublin Industrial Estate, Glasnevin, Dublin,
D11 HP5F

ISBN 978 0702 31015 7

A CIP catalogue record for this book is available from the British Library.

Printed by CPI Group (UK) Ltd, Croydon CR0 4YY
Paper made from wood grown in sustainable forests and other controlled sources.

1 3 5 7 9 10 8 6 4 2

www.scholastic.co.uk

GOOD ENOUGH TO EAT

GINA BLAXILL

SCHOLASTIC

To Rex, whose love of books
I hope will last for ever

NOW

THE RETURN

Everyone knew the dangers of venturing too far into the forest. Gretel's first memory was of being tucked up in the big straw bed she had shared with her twin brother Hansel, their mother bringing stories alive as the wind howled so violently it seemed that the cottage would be torn apart.

"But these are not mere fairy tales," her mother had whispered. "They're real. Fear the forest, little ones."

As Gretel grew out of her childish woollen stockings and into high-necked tunics and sturdy clogs, she realized that her mother was right. Child after child from nearby villages vanished into the forest, never to return. Everyone said the same – if the cold and hunger didn't get you, it would be the wolves or bears, who grew bolder year by year.

And if not animals, it would be Old Esther. The witch. The hag who had once been an ordinary villager, but had fled after committing unspeakable acts, discovered dark magic and buried herself in a creaking cottage at the heart of the forest. Her curses were to blame for failing crops, harsh winters and empty bellies – and the witch was also rumoured to eat the missing children...

The stories crept across Gretel's mind now, as she stumbled through the trees with her brother and Lord Fabian's son. It was barely light enough to see Hansel beside her, let alone pick out a safe path. From behind came the soft tread of Jakob's feet as he followed. Every so often snow dropped from the claw-like branch canopy above, sliding down the back of her neck. Ice crystals clung to her hair. Gretel's feet were so stiff, every step was a battle. Every so often her soles crunched something that didn't feel like dead leaves or twigs. *Bones of the witch's victims*, thought Gretel.

The moon's gleam picked out a pebble in the trail that was

guiding the way back to Westerleen. Gretel released a shaky breath. The pebbles had become scattered since she had last followed them, and at points she had feared they would become lost. Better still, beyond, she could see light. Like a moth, Gretel was drawn towards it. If she was correct, that would be the lantern outside the Haufmanns' cottage. Next to her, she could hear Hansel's ragged breathing. The long hike should have been easy for him, given all the times he'd helped their woodsman father, but he was clearly struggling. She reached out, clasping his arm.

"We will reach home," she whispered. "Keep going."

Hansel didn't reply. Normally it was she who was silent, trudging through the washing or the cooking or whatever endless task came next, while he competed with other boys to see whose arrows hit their target, or bartered with travelling merchants who came with stories of the world beyond the village – a world that Gretel, at least, would probably never see. But then, in the forest everything was different.

"How far?" Jakob called in a low voice. Gretel turned. She could barely see his outline in the poor light.

"We are close," she replied. "But we must be quick."

From some way behind them – at least, Gretel really hoped so – came a faint howl. *If the cold and hunger doesn't get you, forest animals will.* She forced herself to pick up the pace. She wasn't going to let a stupid animal ruin this, not now.

The howl came again. This time much closer. No, not just a howl – multiple howls. A whole pack of animals! Gretel's heart flew into her mouth.

"Run," she gasped. "They can smell us."

Her stiff, frozen legs screamed as she used the last of her energy to put on a burst of speed. Brambles tore at her clothes. The ground dipped and she overbalanced, shoulder pounding against a trunk and knocking the air from her lungs. She staggered up, and on. She could hear the boys running behind her. Gretel chanced a look back. Eyes gleamed through the brambles. Feral, hungry eyes. Gretel's hands flew to her hip but she had no weapons, nothing…

The uneven ground smoothed out. The path! Suddenly there were no trees above them, just a broad, starless sky. Hope swelled inside Gretel. Forest animals never ventured this close to the village. She glanced again over her shoulder. Movement flickered between the trees – shadowy forms slinking back into the forest's dark heart.

Jakob and Hansel joined her. Their breathing sounded very loud in the sudden stillness. Hansel muffled a sob. Gretel's legs felt as though they might snap. She leaned heavily on her brother, gasping. Jakob bent over, resting his hands on his thighs. For a long moment, none of them moved.

"We must go," Gretel whispered when she felt strong enough to speak. They had cleared the forest. A new ordeal awaited them in Westerleen, one Gretel almost feared more: the villagers.

What would Albrect Haufmann and the Neydeckers and the other men whose opinions mattered think when they returned? She'd find out when they reached Albrect's cottage, she supposed. It would surely be obvious to them all who was to blame – her father and stepmother. It wouldn't be the first time they had abandoned their children in the woods. And it was no secret what went on behind closed doors in Gretel's home, with her stepmother Ilse's sharp tongue and her father beaten down by life. Ilse would deny she had anything to do with the twins' disappearance, of course, but would she be believed?

After last time, Gretel suspected not, but she couldn't be certain. And that was why she was afraid.

She pulled her cloak more tightly around her shoulders and stumbled forwards. Hansel took her hand as the light grew closer and brighter. Jakob fell into step beside them. The damp earth felt smooth and safe. Gretel choked back the unexpected urge to weep. Tears were what everyone would expect from a girl, but they weren't getting them, not today. The taunts she'd grown up with for being difficult and unruly and stubborn had done something good – they'd toughened her up.

"Gretel." Her brother's voice wobbled. "I'll never forget this. Never."

There was a nasty taste in her mouth. "I did what I had to."

"Of course." His hand squeezed hers. Gretel gasped in pain, and Hansel let go. "Sorry. Did I hurt you?"

Her fingers were burned raw from the witch's oven, not yet blistered. "No," she lied, and her brother laughed, though it was the nervous, hysterical kind.

"Of course not. Nothing hurts you."

"That's not true, Hansel."

"It appears that way sometimes, that's what I meant. I was the one who was terrified of Mother's stories, do you remember?"

Gretel ignored the emptiness that always opened up inside her when Hansel mentioned their mother. Instead, she concentrated on the lantern.

"I was thinking…" Hansel's voice was stronger now. "Maybe I've not been a very good brother. We've not been close the last few years, have we? You in the house, doing the chores, and me out with Father. I'm not going to forget about you again. I won't let anyone tease you. If your hands scar, I won't let people sneer. I'll make them eat their words."

A permanent reminder of the last few days was the last thing Gretel had wanted. With salve, hopefully her hands would heal.

Finally – *finally* – they stepped into the open. Gretel inhaled a big clean breath of air. It tasted sweet and full of promise.

She caught Jakob's eye. He inclined his head, a silent reminder of their conversation in the witch's cottage. Their agreement.

The Haufmanns' dwelling was similar to the one Gretel's family lived in – low and wooden, windows thin and shuttered, a chicken coop outside. It looked the same as it had two weeks ago, but why would it have changed? *I never thought I would return to Westerleen and yet, here we are,* thought Gretel.

She was steeling herself to knock when the door shot open and little Brida ran out into the snow. Her father followed, red-faced.

"And you can stay out there till you apologize!" he yelled.

How many times had Gretel been shouted at in the same way? Forgetting herself a second, Gretel wrapped an arm around the girl.

"Brida."

Brida's eyes swelled. "Gretel? You're alive!"

"What?" Big Albrect Haufmann was rooted to the spot, jaw hanging open, a funny look on a man who normally strode around the village like a king – which, as Westerleen's leader, he more or less was. "My God! We thought you lost to the forest. Your father denied leaving you there, but we all knew. Come out of the cold, Hansel, quickly. Gretel, too. And – oh." His eyebrows shot upwards as he noticed Jakob. "Lord Fabian's son! Come, come."

His calloused hand grasped Hansel. Gretel followed with Brida and Jakob. In the messy kitchen, Brida's brothers huddled by the fire, sharing slabs of the dense black bread bulked out with empty corn husks. It smelled of wood smoke. Albrect swept the bench clear so Jakob and Hansel could sit and, without waiting to be asked, Gretel sat too. "See to the boys' cuts," Albrecht called to his wife. "And you," he turned to his sons, "get out there and tell their fathers the news."

Gretel could imagine what her father's reaction would be. She almost wished she could watch.

Hansel leaned close. In the candlelight she could see his face, streaked with filth, a mirror of hers. He gave her a watery version of his famous smile, the smile that was hers too. Only while Hansel, with his strong jaw and wide gaze, was considered handsome, she was seen as difficult and stubborn.

"Father won't want us back," he whispered. "He abandoned us."

Gretel pretended to inspect her hands.

"I still can't believe it," Hansel carried on. "I thought he cared. Ilse doesn't, we know that from last time – but Father..."

Last time. Those scars ran deep, deeper than the burns on Gretel's hands would. Outside, she heard shouting: the Haufmann boys, spreading the news.

"How did you escape?" Brida draped a blanket over Gretel's shoulders. "Did the witch try to eat you? Is her house made of gingerbread like they say?"

The front door opened. The family that lived next to the Haufmanns piled in, chattering excitedly. Others raced up behind them. Gretel spotted the Neydecker brothers, who often laughed at her and called her names. She had heard so many taunts that she should be immune, but each remained, like a brand on her skin.

And this is where I have returned to, a place where I am nothing. Gretel realized she was still trembling all over. *I should not have come back. I should have stayed. No, I could not. Will they believe the story of what happened? Or will they dismiss me, and all will go back to how it was before?*

She found she could not speak. Hansel was the one who said it.

"The witch is dead."

Albrect gave a start. His wife, crouched down bathing Hansel's ankles, froze. The remaining Haufmann children went rigid, and the chattering villagers went quiet.

"What?" Albrect bellowed. Everyone's eyes swivelled to Hansel. Albrect smacked Hansel's shoulders, eyes bright. "I knew it. I've always thought you were a better son than your father deserved; always thought you'd do big things. And you brought your sister and the lord's son home safely, too!" He raised his voice. "Hansel has slain the witch!"

Still more villagers were gathering, a good twenty or so now, with others outside. The men who sat with Albrect on the village council muscled their way to the front. Hansel was trying to speak as he rose, holding on to the table for support, but the excited chatter drowned his words. No one was looking Gretel's way. They were all thronging her brother, grasping his hand to shake it. The questions came thick and fast.

"What is inside the house? Did you see evidence of spells? Has she cursed the village?"

"Is it true that the witch is Esther – that she is really one of us?"

"What about the missing children?"

"Why did she take Gretel too, when until now she only took boys?"

"Did she admit to eating them? My Kasper vanished three

years ago, and my sister's boy two months back. We will never stop yearning for answers … never."

"The witch had every intention of eating me." Hansel sounded stronger now. "She kept me and Jakob locked up, made Gretel slave for her – cooking, cleaning, carrying firewood. You would not know there was famine from looking at her pantry – she was fattening us up with cake and gingerbread and meat and cheese." He paused. "All the stories are true."

Hansel really did love an audience. He should be an actor. All Gretel could see were people's backs. They had forgotten she was there.

Again, Jakob's eyes met hers.

"Everyone, quiet!" Albrect bellowed. "This is too much, too loud. We have plenty of time to get the details straight. For now, though – we owe this young man a debt Westerleen can never repay."

He rose from his perch on the bench. Everyone fell silent. Then, Albrect started clapping. The councilmen followed his lead. Ten, twenty – thirty, even – pairs of hands. Applauding her brother. Shouting his name. Faces, wreathed in smiles. Cheering. Children, bright-eyed. Someone had even broken out into a spontaneous jig.

"Hansel, Hansel, Hansel!"

Gretel dug her fingers deep into her palms, right into the burns.

THEN

ONE MONTH EARLIER

"How is it possible for you to be this slow?" snapped Gretel's stepmother. Ilse's foot nudged the wooden bucket Gretel was using to mop the cottage floor. For a moment, Gretel thought she was going to overturn it out of spite. "Good as useless. You may consider yourself too high and mighty for household tasks, but one day soon enough you'll have your own house to run. Then you'll thank me for teaching you how to do things properly."

This again. Gretel gritted her teeth. "There is only one person who considers herself high and mighty, and it's not me."

"Don't you dare answer back."

"I am not answering back. You said something that wasn't true."

Ilse glared at Gretel, hands on hips. A strand of fair hair fell out from under her coif. In the dull afternoon light, the groove between her eyebrows looked even deeper and more disapproving than usual. By Westerleen's standards, their cottage was large – an airy living space with well-worn but sturdy furniture and a deep open fire and, at the back, two small bedrooms with solid straw mattresses that had lasted years.

All reminders of easier times, thought Gretel. Her memories of plentiful food and finer clothes were only faded ones, yet still a familiar ache clamped her chest. Although her father was but a poor woodcutter, her mother had been a merchant's daughter, and, thanks to her dowry, Gretel's early years had been comparatively affluent. Ilse still liked to keep up the pretence of prosperity years on – hence her fastidious cleaning. She wanted to be a somebody. Who Ilse thought she was fooling, Gretel had no idea. It was hard to keep any secrets in a village of Westerleen's size. A rumour had circulated for a time that Gretel's mother had hidden a secret stash of gold somewhere as inheritance for her children, and perhaps some believed it – but most saw the reality. That of a family on the edge.

Gretel watched Ilse's expression sour. She almost wanted her stepmother to explode with anger so she could shout back. Anything to break the endless cycle of mopping and dusting the entire house until her back ached and the dry, chipped skin around her knuckles bled. But Ilse simply huffed and turned back to the stove.

"I will ignore your impudence," she said grandly. "But I shall tell your father."

As though that would get any kind of reaction. Gretel plunged the mop back into the bucket. Grubby water spilled over the side. Her father was accomplished at turning a blind eye to the less pleasant things that went on under his own roof, mostly because he was hardly ever there. When he wasn't deep in the forest with his axe, he was at the inn, placing bets on card games and downing bitter, watery ale. Once upon a time, back when Gretel's mother had been alive, Father had been relaxed and big-hearted, the kind of person whose charisma drew admirers and friends, and who laughed at how lucky he had been to win Mother's heart.

Gretel smacked the mop against the floorboards with such

violence, water splashed her toes. When had her father lost that verve? He had grieved his first wife deeply, but losing her had not broken him – not that Gretel saw, anyway. He had been content enough in the early years after marrying Ilse, just one month after Gretel's mother had been buried. Was it increasingly difficult village life that had ground him down, or the lack of harmony under his own roof? Or did he drink and gamble to forget his hardships?

Not that I care, Gretel thought savagely. She would never forgive him for foisting Ilse upon her and Hansel. They would have been just fine, the three of them. Perhaps they could have left Westerleen with the last of their money and built a new life somewhere else. Somewhere it would have been acceptable for Gretel to do things other than scrub stoves and chop carrots.

"When that floor is shining, you can fetch firewood." Ilse was tidying her hair in the reflection in the window. "The woodshed is running low. Stop by the market, too, before the stalls close."

Ilse liked Gretel to shop at the end of the day, when the merchants wanted to get rid of their stock and charged less. Everyone was growing desperate these days.

She worked in silence as Ilse sliced onions and potatoes, attempting to stretch the skinny chicken she had plucked bare into something resembling a substantial meal. Ilse's hands were as dry and worn as Gretel's, a far cry from the soft, fine skin and beautiful nails Gretel remembered from years ago, when Ilse had merely been her mother's beguiling best friend.

Her mother. Something lodged in Gretel's throat. Why was she thinking of her so much today? To Gretel's horror, she could feel her eyes watering. She scrubbed them dry and tried as best she could to empty her head. She could not afford to indulge in tender memories.

As quickly as possible, Gretel finished the mopping and poured the dirty water into the undergrowth outside. The chilly air immediately cleared her head. She grabbed a basket from the woodshed.

"Don't dawdle," Ilse called as the door swung shut behind Gretel.

Gretel rolled her eyes. "*Don't dawdle*," she mimicked. She would take as long as she pleased. If Ilse scolded her, so be it.

She thought of Hansel, out with their father and thus escaping the sharpest barbs and put-downs. Lucky Hansel.

Gretel headed down the dirt track that led to what passed for the centre of Westerleen – though really it was just a wide road with space for market stalls, a scattering of shops and an inn. Most people lived on farms or in cottages up dirt tracks within ten minutes' walk. Once, Westerleen had been vibrant, welcoming new families and tradesfolk, swelling into a small town. That growth had stalled and died a few decades ago. Little wonder. No one wanted to build a life somewhere children vanished in the trees, never to return...

Gretel's stomach rumbled. The breakfast of watery porridge she'd tried to consume as slowly as possible had been hours ago. The scrappy bread roll that had been lunch barely counted. She instead concentrated on avoiding the worst of the mud. The basket bumped her hip. *I could do this walk blindfolded,* thought Gretel. She could do *everything* blindfolded. Clean. Cook. Tidy. Clean again.

She rounded the corner, and there was Hansel with his friends, lounging against the wall of the Neydeckers' cottage as they often did when they were not at work alongside their fathers. As far as Gretel could tell, they did precious little with their spare time except play card games, shoot arrows or occasionally fish.

"I spy your sister, Hansel." Wonderful – they'd noticed her. "And no surprise, she's looking sulky. Would it hurt to smile?"

Gretel looked up sharply but couldn't tell which boy had spoken. His voice was purposefully loud enough for her to hear. Since when had taunting her become a sport? Hansel murmured something and half-smiled, picking at the frayed cuff to his jerkin. Of course, he didn't defend her.

Rudolf Neydecker picked up the taunting. "Poor Cristoph, promised to the most miserable girl in Westerleen. He should break the betrothal. Everyone would understand."

"He'll never do that," said Rudolf's brother, Siegfried. "Cristoph believes in her mother's mythical fortune! He is a fool who cannot see her father has gambled it all away. If it ever existed."

"Stop it," Hansel mumbled. His feeble objection was drowned out by his friends' laughter.

Do not get involved, Gretel told herself as she clomped past. *Imagine you are as deaf as old Mistress Fischer. Imagine you are a horse with blinkers. Do not feel. Do not stick up for yourself. Do not make things worse.*

She had repeated the words to herself so many times over the years that it was easy to slip into a trance.

Hansel caught up with her as she neared the marketplace.

"Are you going to the market?"

Gretel rolled her eyes. "Where else would I be going?"

"To see a friend? I don't know."

How did he still not understand what she did all day? Why couldn't Hansel fetch logs, or haggle with merchants? He would do a better job than her. People were drawn to his relaxed, easy manner in a way they weren't to Gretel, who was impatient and cross.

Normally Gretel managed to control herself but today her feelings spilled into words. "I don't have time to see friends, Hansel. Chores do not do themselves. Why don't you help? Bring more logs home from the forest, for instance. It is ridiculous that I have to keep fetching wood from the village shed, and I cannot carry as much as you could. My arms ache from Ilse's ridiculous scrubbing."

Hansel fell into step beside her. "Don't snap at me, Gretel. You speak as though I have been idle all day and I haven't. When I'm not chopping wood, we're building and repairing houses. That's tiring work, especially on an empty stomach. It isn't as though I have it easy either."

Maybe not – after all, he did work hard – but Hansel had been outside, breathing clean air and listening to birdsong. Now he could relax with his horrible friends. In a few years, when he was no longer an apprentice, Hansel could leave Westerleen if he wanted and never look back. Gretel could never leave. *And of course, he is ambivalent about it all,* Gretel thought, mood blackening further. *If only we could switch places!*

Hansel dropped his voice.

"I know Rudolf and Siegfried were being unkind, Gretel. But you bring it upon yourself. If you were more agreeable, they would leave you alone."

"Who decides what agreeable is?" Gretel shot back. "Them? And how *can* you sit there and smile while they mock Mother?"

Hansel looked flustered. "They aren't mocking her. They are mocking the silly story about her secret treasure trove. Look, you aren't really angry because of me. Is it Ilse? Is she being especially unpleasant?"

Some of Gretel's anger fizzled out. As annoyed as she was with Hansel, he was the only person who knew what it was like at home. "She is insufferable. How Father let himself be tricked into marrying her, I do not know."

Hansel gave her a sideways look. "We don't know if she tricked him."

She did, thought Gretel. *She must have.* Their mother had barely been cold before Ilse took over the house, changing everything, and telling Father what to do. Even when Mother was dying, Ilse was there, cooking rabbit stew and letting him cry into her shoulder.

"I think she believed in Mother's hidden fortune herself and that's why she made herself so indispensable. Well, the joke is on her."

Hansel sighed, raking a hand through his hair, the exact same corn colour as Gretel's. Like most Westerleen boys and men, he wore it shoulder-length. "I don't like her any more than you do, but there is nothing we can do, is there?"

"We could put poisonous forest mushrooms in her stew," muttered Gretel. "That would solve the problem."

"Gretel! No. Don't even think about it! If— Wait." Hansel smiled. "You are joking."

"Am I?"

"Yes, because you know it wouldn't work. Everyone would know you had done it and cast you out with nothing, and that would almost certainly mean death." Irritatingly, Hansel was right. He continued. "Try not to let her upset you. Raging doesn't help. You'll get married to Cristoph and have a house of your own to run before too long, and then you never need speak to Ilse again."

Gretel shot him an incredulous look. "Is that supposed to comfort me?"

"Yes." Hansel looked baffled. "You are old enough to marry, just about. Ilse's been saying to her friends that it will happen soon."

Gretel stopped so suddenly she almost tripped. "What?"

"If you spent more time with other people, you'd know that

already," said Hansel. "Has it not even crossed your mind? The sooner you are someone else's responsibility, the sooner there is one less mouth to feed." He tilted his face upwards. "Hmm. I think it might snow."

Gretel couldn't care less about snow. She grasped his wrist. "What else did Ilse say?"

"Only that the Spring Festival would be a good time."

The Spring Festival was just months away. Dread twisted Gretel's belly, so visceral she felt sick. The betrothal between her and Cristoph had been arranged many years ago – and yet somehow, she had never believed it would come to anything.

It was a good match for her. Cristoph came from one of Westerleen's more prosperous and influential families, and that opened up better prospects than Gretel could reasonably have hoped for. She should, by rights, be looking forward to it. But how could she, when marriage would mean she became Cristoph's property, and completely beholden to him?

I am only fifteen! she thought. Weddings this young did happen, but mostly amongst the nobles. Gretel had been depending on Ilse being in no rush to formalize matters – who else would scrub her precious floor? – but clearly she had misjudged her stepmother.

"Please tell me you are making this up, Hansel," she said in a small voice.

Her brother shook her head. "Speak to Ilse about it, not me. Better still, ask Cristoph."

"He is the last person I will be speaking to. Perhaps he will come to his senses and call our promise off."

"It could be much worse," said Hansel. "And it will be if Ilse has anything to do with it. I saw Heinrich Mulch leaving our house last week. Everyone knows he is looking to marry again."

"Heinrich Mulch? He's older than Father! He needs a nurse, not a wife." Panic filled Gretel as she pictured herself tending to the old man night and day, enduring his endless hacking cough and rancid breath, emptying his bed pan. Even dull and sanctimonious Cristoph was better than that! Ilse had no reason to seek another match for Gretel, so Heinrich Mulch must have approached her. He was as well-off as Cristoph's family, even more so, perhaps. What if he made an offer for Gretel that Ilse couldn't refuse?

The market came into view. Hansel stopped to greet two children, crouching down to their level so they could show him their toys. Gretel turned away, biting her lip so hard she tasted blood.

I shouldn't have been so impudent to Ilse, she thought. *She has the power to ruin me. Perhaps I can sweeten her up, get on her good side… She might empathize. She's ambitious, clever. We have more in common than we do not.*

Something cold and wet specked her nose.

"There you go!" said Hansel. "I was right. First snow of the cold season."

Gretel frowned. "It is early for snow."

"Another sign that a harsh winter is coming." Hansel's eyes met Gretel's. "Do you think…?"

"Think what?"

He swallowed, his Adam's apple bobbing. Suddenly he looked vulnerable. "They won't do it again, will they? Father and Ilse, I mean. No matter how bad things get, they won't do it again?"

The question hung in the air as ominously as the dark clouds clustering above them. As one, the twins turned, gazing in the direction of the forest. Suddenly it was three years ago. Gretel was twelve again. Her hand was in Father's, being led deep into the darkness, branches stretching over her like a death shroud. She could hear his words even now: *I don't want to do this, but I have no choice. On the other side of the forest are towns and villages. You must find your way there, Hansel and Gretel. Someone will take pity and help you…*

Just the memory made her go cold.

Gretel reached out and gave her brother's hand a quick squeeze. "It does no good to think about it."

"How can we not?" cried Hansel. "Father is cowed by Ilse, and she hates us. If food runs low and we become desperate again…"

He stopped as Mistress Meier, the innkeeper's wife, passed by, calling out hello and lingering to remark on the weather. She addressed herself to Hansel rather than Gretel. It seemed once you got a reputation for being disagreeable, you became invisible.

When they were alone again, Hansel lowered his voice. "Gretel, marry Cristoph … and soon. Ilse will have no power over you then. What choice do you really have?"

None, and Gretel knew it. She had no money, no skills and no power. She had nothing. Hansel did care and, in his way, he tried to look out for her – but he didn't understand. Westerleen felt smaller than ever before – the ramshackle cottages and mud and snow closing around her. The dark, dangerous forest the twins had been fortunate to escape from before almost seemed to be whispering to Gretel: *we won't let go of you a second time.*

NOW

THE RETURN

"Everyone, please." Albrect held up a hand. The way he stood, straight-backed and legs apart, reminded Gretel of her father. Her father, who would know by now that his children had returned from the forest a second time. "You will get the chance to ask your questions, but the twins are exhausted," Albrect was saying. "They need rest, not interrogation. For now, go home, and spread the joyful news. We need never fear the witch again!"

This elicited more cheers. The villagers were reluctant to move.

Albrect and a couple of other men had to herd them away like cattle. Little wonder. This was the most exciting thing that had happened to Westerleen in years. Possibly ever.

Gretel stared at Hansel, so hard she was amazed he could not feel it. Surely he would tell the true story in a moment. He couldn't let them carry on heralding him as a hero. Could he?

She caught Hansel's eye and her brother looked away. Gretel's jaw tightened. If he wouldn't tell the truth then she must. Yet her body was starting to sag. She hadn't realized quite how exhausted she was until this moment – not just in her body, but her mind, too. It was getting harder to think straight. She opened her mouth but then Albrect's wife was there, gently guiding Gretel to the rocking chair by the fire. Brida drew a woollen blanket over her, tucking it in at the edges as though Gretel were an infant in need of swaddling.

"There." Albrect finally managed to close the door. Only a handful of men remained; respected figures who, along with Albrect, ran the village. They formed a circle around Gretel, Jakob and Hansel, blocking out the light. Gretel felt suddenly small and exposed. Albrect squatted so he could look the young people in the eye.

"I could not be happier that you are all back in Westerleen

safely." He paused. "Jakob, I am sure that your father will be equally delighted. Perhaps, in gratitude, he might consider providing the village with the aid we badly need to survive winter. If you could stress to him how fearful we are of the coming months, we would all appreciate it."

Albrect's tone was respectful but firm. Gretel half-expected Jakob to come out with something flippant, but he just nodded. Albrect turned to the other men.

"In the morning, we must dispatch a group to the witch's cottage and see what there is to find," he said. "We deserve answers, to be able to grieve our children properly."

"Our sons," corrected Ludwig Neydecker, expression stony.

"Yes," Albrect said. "Sons. Would you know why the witch only ever took boys? I assume she wanted Gretel as a servant."

He directed the question at Hansel and Jakob. Hansel wet his lips.

"Gretel was the one the witch spoke to," he murmured.

Albrect's gaze pivoted to Gretel. "Well?"

Gretel instinctively dipped her eyes, the way a good Westerleen girl was supposed to.

"Esther kept me cooking and cleaning." No – she should not use her name. *The witch* was safer, it made it clear there was a distance between them. "The witch did not share her secrets with me."

"I suppose you want to know my secrets," said Esther.

She sat in her rocking chair by the kitchen hearth, adorned in the plain black gown she always wore. Wiry white curls fell almost to her waist. Her face was heavily lined, her eyes beady as they squinted at Gretel. Gretel had no idea how old she was and did not dare ask.

Esther's vast oven filled the room with warmth. Even though the only thing inside was gingerbread, there was an underlying bitterness to the smell of baking that put Gretel in mind of cooking meat. Or maybe it was her imagination. Either way, she preferred not to dwell on it.

Gretel did not answer Esther for a long moment, concentrating instead on the large saucepan she had spent the last ten minutes scrubbing. She had been trying not to think about what might have been boiled inside that, either.

"It depends which secrets you are offering to share with me," she said. "I know well enough the fate you have in mind for my brother."

"Ah, but do you?" Esther leaned forwards, the glasses she

sometimes perched on her nose glinting in the candlelight. As far as Gretel could discern, they had no positive effect on the witch's failing eyesight at all.

Gretel wasn't sure if Esther was trying to trick her, but answered anyway. "You kidnap Westerleen boys – those foolish or desperate enough to wander into the forest. You cook them and eat them. I have heard the stories. And then there is that." She gestured to the oven.

Esther smiled slowly, the exact same time as her rocking chair creaked.

"All you have seen me baking is gingerbread."

"You are keeping my brother and the lord's son in cells and feeding them until they are fit to burst. What other possible reason could you have for doing that?"

"If I eat the boys, dear Gretel, why am I so skinny?" A pause. "If you are a good girl, you'll soon find out…"

Albrect's wife poked the fire, and Gretel jumped. Ludwig Neydecker was saying something. She had to ask him to repeat it.

"You called the witch Esther. It is true, then, that is who she is?"

Gretel nodded. Albrect closed his eyes.

"I have always wondered," he said. "My grandmother remembered Esther well. For years she was an ordinary housewife.

Why she turned to evil, well … it is a mystery. I suppose she learned dark magic in the forest."

"So you weren't locked up?" asked Ludwig of Gretel. "The witch had you doing chores?"

Gretel nodded again.

"Then why didn't you attempt to run back to Westerleen and seek help?" Ludwig didn't look disbelieving, exactly, but there was a sternness there that worried Gretel.

Luckily, she had her answer ready. "And abandon my brother? I couldn't."

Ludwig nodded. "Your loyalty does you credit."

What about loyalty to Esther, who had opened her eyes and taught her so much?

Hansel spoke. "Gretel did what she could to protect us. The witch kept pinching our fingers, to determine if we were fat enough to cook. Her eyesight was poor. Gretel would slip us chicken bones to stick through the bars and trick the witch."

"Clever idea, Hansel," said one of the men, giving him an approving nod. Gretel recalled plucking apart the chicken carcass, selecting the bones that were most likely to deceive the witch and persuading Hansel the ruse was worth trying. Her numbness returned.

Albrect lowered his voice. "This is difficult to ask, but your father will be here shortly. We need to know the truth." A pause. "The two of you entering the forest. Was this a repeat of three years ago?"

Gretel felt rather than saw Hansel flinch.

"It was our idea," he mumbled. "We thought we'd have a better life if we could reach the villages on the other side of the forest. Father didn't know anything, he..." Hansel trailed off. His face, which had turned a funny green colour, might as well have had "liar" written all over it.

A dark look passed between the men.

"Your father promised us this would not happen again, not even in the harshest times," said Albrect. "He swore an oath. He told us you had taken the road from Westerleen, heading south to seek your fortune. A lie."

Hansel's shoulders slumped. He didn't argue. Westerleen, for all its faults, was a strong community where families stuck together, and where children – even those nearing adulthood – obeyed parents without question if they lived under the same roof.

Three years ago. Gretel closed her eyes...

THEN

THREE YEARS AGO

The inner walls of the cottage were thin, meaning twelve-year-old Gretel could overhear Ilse and her father's whispered conversations after dark almost word for word. She lay under the thick covers, straining to follow the words over Hansel's soft snoring from the other end of the bed.

"… the situation cannot continue." That was Ilse. "There is no way we can survive this winter if your children remain in the house. We simply cannot provide for them as well as ourselves. I have begged our neighbours for help, but they are unable to spare any more food."

"I am trying my hardest." Gretel's father sounded helpless, as he so often did in conversations with Ilse. "All week, I have spent hours in the forest, hunting, but only have one rabbit to show for it. Perhaps if I venture deeper into the trees, I may have better luck…"

"That seems unlikely. No, the problem is Hansel and Gretel."

Gretel stiffened.

"Growing children have such mighty appetites," Ilse continued. "They deserve full bellies. If we cannot give them what they need, it really would be a kindness to let them seek a life elsewhere."

The words hung. Ilse's voice oozed concern. If Gretel had not known Ilse better, she would have believed she really cared.

"What are you suggesting?" asked Father, after a long pause. "Neither of us have any family. There is nowhere for them to go."

"But there is, my love." Something creaked. Gretel imagined Ilse shifting to stare at her father with her hard, icy eyes.

"Ilse. Don't."

"You love the children, I know, and I would not contemplate suggesting this if it were not a matter of life and death, but … there are villages other than Westerleen, Georg. Towns, even. Places they could reach on foot, places that will be better homes to two bright children in the years that come. Mathilde wanted them to do things with their lives, didn't she? This could even be an opportunity." She paused. "If they can only find their way through the forest..."

"It's too dangerous," Father said immediately. "They're twelve. Trekking through the trees would take days, even if they knew the right direction in which to head."

"Hansel is a capable enough hunter. He will look after Gretel." A pause. "We wouldn't be the first family to leave children in the forest. It used to be quite common when we were growing up, do you remember?"

"That does not mean it should happen now."

"Everyone would sympathize, Georg. Some of them may even be having this very same conversation, right now."

Hansel made a snorting noise, stirring, and Ilse and Father went silent. Gretel cursed, and kicked Hansel's side. He grunted, turned over and settled. Gretel waited, barely breathing.

"Still asleep," said Ilse, and Gretel closed her eyes in relief. "We need to make a decision, my love. Very soon."

"I cannot let my children go." Father sounded tearful. "I promised Mathilde I would look after them. A deathbed promise, Ilse."

"Mathilde would understand." Ilse's voice turned hard. "If

they stay here, they might not survive the winter. By letting them go you would be looking after them, just as promised. You do see that, don't you?"

"Perhaps you're right," mumbled Father. "God have mercy on us."

Gretel's insides turned to ice. He really was considering it. Ilse had turned his head with her clever words. For the first time, Gretel saw it plainly. Her father was weak. He would defer to Ilse because it was easiest. Even if it meant betraying the memory of his first wife – and his living children.

The conversation died down after that. Gretel lay staring at the ceiling. Sleep was impossible. Her heart was pounding. She had heard stories of children being led into the forest and abandoned in the hopes that they would find a better life elsewhere. They never heard the ending to those stories. No one knew if the children ever reached these towns and villages that were supposedly full of promise. More likely, these wretched boys and girls wandered in circles in the forest until they either starved, died of exhaustion, or were devoured by wolves, bears and whatever animals lurked in its depths.

And then of course there was the witch. Only two weeks ago, Hansel's friend Kasper had vanished while hunting. Even his family had all but given up searching.

Was the situation really as dire as Ilse made out? It was true that each day their stomachs rumbled, but had Ilse really asked their neighbours for food? Gretel somehow found it hard to picture Ilse knocking on doors and begging for help. She was too fond of acting the grand lady. Could that have been a lie?

I cannot depend on Father any more, thought Gretel, and something hardened inside her. The only person she could rely on was herself.

Hansel shifted again. Such a restless sleeper! Gretel was sure Mother would be horrified if she knew that they were still sharing a bed aged twelve, because her father could not afford to have a new mattress made. Hansel was not someone she could rely upon either, much as their father would like to convince himself otherwise. Her brother was a fair hunter, it was true, but under pressure he tended to crumble. And he idolized his father. Hansel would not believe her when she told him what she had overheard, Gretel was sure. He'd say she was dreaming, or making things up because she resented Ilse.

No, it was up to her, and her alone.

The next morning, the family sat around the table chewing the dry, heavy bread that was supposed to keep them going until the sun went down. Today its texture was so coarse that Gretel thought it might choke her. As usual, Gretel's task was to lay out food and collect water from the well. On days when there was hot food, she would cook and serve porridge and clean the pot before eating her own breakfast, which was one of Ilse's rules. By then it would be lukewarm at best, and everyone else would have finished. The one time she had complained, Ilse had said smartly, "It is your job to ensure everyone else is comfortable, Gretel, so quieten down and be a good girl."

Gretel watched her father and Ilse closely. Perhaps it was the way the bright early morning light fell through the window and gleamed off her hair, but her stepmother looked almost ... radiant. As though energized by the prospect of ridding herself of the stepchildren she detested.

In contrast, Father was hunched and miserable, wearing an empty expression that was too familiar these days. Was he thinking of Mother and how badly he had let her down, squandering the money she had left on cards and dice?

All day Gretel stayed vigilant, expecting the worst. Nothing happened. It was an ordinary day: Father went into the woods, Hansel accompanying him, and Ilse ordered Gretel about, though her tongue was noticeably less sharp than usual. *Maybe, just maybe*, Gretel thought, as she lay down that night, exhausted, *Father has reconsidered…*

"Gretel." Shaking roused her from slumber. It was Ilse, candle in hand, fully dressed despite the blackness outside. Hansel was sitting up and rubbing his eyes, hair tufted upwards.

"Get dressed," Ilse said, and left. Gretel's heart thudded against her ribcage.

"What's going on?" said Hansel sleepily. She couldn't answer. It was happening.

Downstairs, Father stood with a knapsack in hand. Haltingly, voice shaking, he announced that he was leading the twins into the forest. Hansel stared at him, eyes big and unblinking. His jaw hung open.

In contrast, Gretel was numb. She felt Ilse's eyes on her, daring her to fight. Gretel looked away. Arguing would achieve nothing. But she would not meekly accept her fate. A sudden idea came to her.

"May I go and bid goodbye to the hen?" she asked.

"How sentimental." Ilse sounded almost amused. "That bird's purpose is to lay eggs, not be petted, but as you wish, Gretel."

Silently Gretel stole outside. Quickly she collected as many pebbles from the path as she could, stowing them in the deep pockets of her cape.

Minutes later, Gretel, Hansel and their father were trudging into the trees, having bid goodbye to Ilse, who had wrung her hands in a fake display of grief that made Gretel's lip curl in disgust. The sun was yet to rise. No one would be around for several hours. *The perfect time to abandon your children,* thought Gretel, wiping the tears that stung her eyes.

She hung back as their feet crunched the hard, frosted mud, letting Father and Hansel take the lead. Every twenty steps, her fingers closed around a new pebble, which she dropped to the ground.

They walked through the forest. The well-trodden path ended, giving way to twigs and leaves. Gretel had never gone this far before. Still, they travelled deeper. The trees thickened. By the time Father stopped, Gretel's feet ached. The sky was beginning to lighten. They must have been trekking for a couple of hours, maybe more. Father took a deep breath, then turned to the twins.

"I will leave you here. Hansel, you have your bow and your knife. Use them. Gretel, in the knapsack is as much food and water as we could spare. Head towards the rising sun. I cannot claim to know the forest beyond this point, but if you walk straight, your chance of reaching the other side will be greater."

Our chance of not dying, you mean. Gretel allowed her father to hug her, suppressing the part of her that wanted to scream that she was his little girl, and how could he do something so monstrous?

Father faded into the blackness. Gretel thought about following, but the trees were so dense she was scared they would lose him, and she could not leave Hansel alone. Her brother was staring in the direction their father had instructed them to head, motionless. His bow hung limply at his side. After a long moment, he sat down heavily on a tree stump. "How big is the forest, Gretel?"

Too big for two children to survive for long. "We aren't going into the forest, Hansel." Gretel tried to sound confident and reassuring. "We are going home."

"How?" Hansel sounded as though he was struggling not to cry. "I don't know the way. Even woodsmen say the forest is a maze."

"We won't get lost. I have laid a trail. Once the sun rises properly, we will be able to follow it." Gretel nudged the pebble at her feet. And, sure enough, once there was light, the pebbles shone, lighting the way like a line of welcoming candles. Even Gretel was taken aback by how well her plan had worked. Only a couple of times did the twins have to stop and search for the next pebble to show them the right way. Gretel kept alert for the tread or snarls of forest animals, but all was silent.

By late afternoon, Westerleen came into view. If she had not been so exhausted, Gretel would have laughed at Ilse's expression when the twins walked through the cottage door. One of the hens Gretel had pretended to be so attached to lay on the table, plucked and ready for roasting, and there were clean, firm carrots and also a potato. Hardly a fine meal, but glorious compared to the stale biscuits and crusts the family had been surviving on. Almost ... *celebratory.*

Gretel did not know what to believe. Was it possible her stepmother had been exaggerating how dire the situation was to Father? Surely no one would be that cold, or so ruthless.

If it was true... Ilse wanted them gone. And she did not care how.

In the end, little was said about the twins' miraculous return. Disturbingly little, in fact. Their father cried when he opened the door soon after and saw his children, and his warmth as he embraced Hansel then Gretel appeared genuine. But from the calculating way Ilse watched them, Gretel knew that unless she acted first, within days they would be abandoned again. And this time there would be no bidding farewell to hens.

There was only one thing she could think to do. Once, Gretel would rather have gone hungry than betray her family, but she bore her father and Ilse no loyalty any more. They were the enemy. When you had no power, you had to strike first to triumph. Her mother's stories of far-flung battles and heroes defying the odds had taught her that.

While Ilse was cooking, Gretel took Hansel's hand and led him to The Green Gate, Westerleen's sole inn, where the men gathered as the sun set. There, she found Albrect Haufmann, Ludwig Neydecker and the other important men. A woodsman spotted them first and fell silent. One by one, the men turned. Knowing she would not be believed if she spoke, Gretel remained silent, praying that the dry leaves and cobwebs still clinging to her plaits and Hansel's torn, grubby tunic would tell their own story. Sure enough, Albrect said, "Hansel, what has happened?"

Gretel nudged his shin with her foot, urging him to play his part. Hansel did not hesitate. The whole story poured out, accompanied by tears. If there was one thing her brother could be relied on to do, it was to give a real performance. The men's expressions went tight with barely concealed anger.

"You did the right thing, coming to us," Albrect's voice was as ominous as a storm cloud. "What your father and stepmother tried to do is not something I will stand for. I was one of ten once.

My parents took my youngest brother and sister into the forest." For a moment, his voice caught. "I will never know exactly what fate befell them. We are better than that now. We stand together; we do not sacrifice the vulnerable." He stood, banging his fist on the table. Like Hansel, Albrect appreciated an audience. At least he followed his grand speeches with action, which could not be said for all Westerleen men and boys. "Times are difficult but no one will starve in Westerleen. Not if we band together."

The men downed their ale and marched out. With any luck, they would find Ilse still preparing her feast – Gretel would love to know how her stepmother would attempt to explain that! The twins were taken aside and fed watery broth that tasted heavenly despite really being only coloured water. Mistress Meier fussed over them and kept saying Ilse only needed to ask for help, and that there was no shame in being poor. So Ilse had lied about that.

Gretel did not know what Albrect and the men said to her father and Ilse but from that point onwards, there was enough food on the table for the family to survive and no more attempts were made to take the twins into the trees. Father stopped joining his friends at the inn, and it was only many months later that he was welcomed back. Ilse's lips were permanently pursed. Most days she could barely even look at Gretel. The atmosphere inside the cottage was permanently sour and it made Gretel anxious. When the twins went out into the village, everyone would check they were being properly looked after.

And – curiously – people also started clapping Hansel on the back. They would congratulate him for guiding Gretel home, and call him clever. Hansel looked as baffled as Gretel at first but, after it had happened several times, his chest puffed out and he gained confidence. He started to say things like "I couldn't let us be abandoned" and "I promised Mother I'd look after my sister."

Gretel watched open-mouthed. Had Hansel actually started to believe this? When Hansel had first spilled the story, he had been truthful enough about her being the one to lay the pebble trail. His voice had been muffled, and the men had told him to stop and breathe a couple of times, but Gretel had thought him clear enough.

Had the story become confused as it spread through Westerleen? *No*, thought Gretel. She could accept that one man might mistake who had done what, but not a dozen. They had all, somehow, rearranged the story in their heads so that Hansel was the one whose sharp thinking had saved the twins and not she. Because he was a boy. It was … laughable. Hansel was agreeable, not bold, and he followed Gretel's lead, happy to let her do the thinking. He was the first to fall for even the most far-fetched practical joke, and even Mother, who had loved him whole-heartedly, had once said, "Oh, my dear boy, you are not much of a thinker, are you?"

Didn't everyone see that? Or did they not want to see?

Gretel's heart was so hard by now it might as well have been one of the pebbles that had saved her. She knew she should not allow the villagers' false beliefs to bother her. She and Hansel were alive and Ilse would find it a challenge to play any more dirty tricks. That was what mattered.

All the same, Gretel burned with the unfairness of it all. And, as the years passed, that fire only burned more fiercely.

NOW

HOME AGAIN

The Morning After the Return

At first, Gretel could not work out where she was when she awoke with a stiff, aching back and cold air circling her bare feet. Then it sunk in: she was no longer on Esther's soft feather mattress. She was home, on the lumpy straw mattress that passed for her bed, blanket half-on, half-off. She had fallen asleep almost instantly, exhausted from the fraught dash through the forest, then the volley of questions in the Haufmanns' cottage.

Gretel stretched out, taking a moment to absorb the familiar noises. Hansel, snoring from behind the wooden screen their father had finally put together to allow the twins some privacy, on the newer, superior mattress. Creaking from the end of the corridor, indicating that Ilse was busy within the kitchen. Less early morning birdsong than she liked, but that was always the same in winter.

It wasn't a dream. It had happened. Every single moment of it.

And now the next chapter of the story began.

I hope I am ready for it.

"Hansel," she said, in a low voice. "Wake up."

Grunting sounded behind the screen, then soft crunching as her brother turned. Gretel rose, pulling the blanket around her shoulders, and peeked around the screen. Hansel blinked at her, all tousled hair and sleepy eyes. Then he rocketed upright.

"The oven – she is going to eat me!"

"The witch is dead, Hansel. You're home. Take a deep breath."

But Hansel was scrabbling about for the knife he kept next to his bed and didn't hear. Gretel discarded her blanket and grasped his shoulders, giving him a firm shake.

"Hansel. Wake up."

Her brother's eyes went big. Then he released a shaky breath. "I was half in a dream."

Gretel hugged him. "It's all right. You're safe now, I promise."

They stayed there a moment before Gretel let go. She spied Hansel's jerkin on the floor. She bent down, picked it up and tossed it on to his bed. "We'd best get ready. I imagine Lord Fabian will want to speak to us today. He will have been reunited with Jakob by now."

She and Hansel had not stayed in the Haufmanns' cottage long enough last night to see Jakob's father, which was probably for the best. The very idea of speaking to the lord who governed the entire region, in all his finery and authority, made Gretel's insides knot. She wanted to have her full wits about her, and energy to draw on.

How would he feel knowing a lowly peasant had saved his son's life? By rights, Lord Fabian should be delighted. The two times she had seen him before he had looked both severe and stern, but he had turned Westerleen upside down trying to find Jakob when he had gone missing. Gretel couldn't imagine her father showing half that determination. She should, therefore, be looking forward to her and Hansel being summoned, and being thanked. So why was her chest so tight? Because of the reception last night, and how swiftly Hansel had been deemed the hero? Or because of the warning Jakob had given her in the cottage?

Gretel, my father isn't the kind of person who changes the way of things. Take it from someone who knows. I'm sorry.

Gretel didn't want to think about that, not now. Jakob had to be wrong. The tightness across her chest was anticipation, not anxiety. She ducked around the screen and opened the chest where she kept her clothes. She wished she had something finer than the faded moss-coloured gown that had never really suited her and had been repaired so many times patches of cloth had worn thin.

Was Jakob awake? She hoped he was all right. There hadn't been a chance to talk to him alone last night, and he hadn't said much in Albrect's cottage. That should be reassuring, but it wasn't. Gretel was uncomfortably aware that she didn't know Jakob, not really. All his talk of deals and agreements and wanting to help her in Esther's cottage could have been bluster. He had needed her then. He didn't any more.

Perhaps she might be able to get Jakob alone after seeing Lord Fabian. Before then, however, she needed to endure something she both dreaded and relished: facing Ilse. Her stepmother had not been present when her father had arrived at the Haufmanns' cottage last night. His expression had been disturbed, and he'd kept looking at Gretel as though she was someone he did not recognize.

Would he tell Ilse everything – including the real reason Hansel and Gretel had been abandoned a second time? Father had a sharp enough mind when it was not befuddled by ale. Gretel's palms turned clammy. She didn't think he would talk, but it wasn't a certainty. The only thing that was certain was that Ilse would be plotting. Ilse was always plotting. Gretel must be on her guard. Today, there would be even more questions.

Including difficult ones.

I will not be numb, Gretel told herself. *I will speak up, even if it is hard. One way or another, the truth will come out.*

She stood up straight, tried to channel the power she had sometimes felt while with Esther, and opened the door.

Father and Ilse were seated with their heads close together, carrying out a hushed conversation, when the twins pushed open the door to the kitchen. They didn't notice the twins at first. Gretel placed a hand on Hansel's arm, raising her finger to her lips, but Hansel spoke loudly.

"We're here."

Father and Ilse broke apart. Immediately, Father glanced away, as though he couldn't bear to behold the children he had probably started to think of as dead. Once, that would have devastated Gretel. Maybe her heart was still pebble-hard, or perhaps someone could only let you down so many times before you stopped expecting anything of them.

"Twins." Father cleared his throat. "Hello. Did you, er... Have you... Please sit."

Nervous. Well, that was no surprise. Gretel crossed the room and drew out a chair, the screech on the uneven tiles slicing into the heavy atmosphere. Gretel didn't offer to prepare anyone's breakfast, or head out to fetch water. And no one ordered her to do so. A curious thrill passed through Gretel. For a long moment there was uncertainty, no one quite sure what roles they ought to be playing any more. Then, without a word, Ilse grabbed the wooden pitcher, face like thunder. The front door thumped behind her.

"There's porridge," mumbled Father, waving at the stove. He waited for Hansel to get up, then leaned close so only Gretel could hear. "I am sorry that your plan went so wrong."

"I don't know what you mean." Gretel kept her expression blank.

Her father frowned. "The evening before you went into the forest, you told me—"

"The night before you abandoned us in the forest," corrected Gretel.

Fear flashed across their father's face. "I did not abandon you. You know that, Gretel."

"Didn't you? You woke Hansel and me up and walked with

52

us into the trees, then said goodbye. Most people would agree you left us there."

Father stuttered, gaping like a fish out of water. "But, we spoke – you said..."

Gretel rose. Inside, she was shaky, but she knew she needed to act with confidence and build on his fear. "The only conversation I recall that evening happened when you were heady with ale. You misremember."

She turned smartly and went to the stove. Despite eating last night, Gretel's stomach growled. She could feel her father's eyes boring into her back as she ladled the sloppy mixture into a wooden bowl. It was nothing like the rich, creamy porridge she had grown accustomed to at Esther's.

"Are you not even going to look at us?" Hansel asked from behind her, voice wounded. Gretel froze. Her brother was angry. And when Hansel was angry, he lost his head.

"What is there to say?" mumbled Father.

"Everything!" hissed Hansel. "You abandoned us, and lied to us! What did you imagine would happen in the forest? Well, Father?"

Gretel's heart pounded faster. Her father hesitated for a long moment. Then, he said, "Please do not rebuke me, Hansel. No one intended for you to be captured by the witch."

Gretel's knees went soft with relief. But when she turned, Hansel was leaning forwards across the table, body language unusually stubborn.

"You must have known the witch might find us."

"The intention was that you would both be safe. There are villages and towns over the other side of the forest. You were supposed to reach them."

"That is what you claimed last time. Another lie. Those places are near impossible to reach by foot. The witch took Gretel to one of the towns on horseback." Hansel leaned further forwards, so his face was just inches from his father's. He was taller than him now, though not as broad. "You never believed we would survive, and you wanted rid of us. I thought you were better than that."

Father shifted. He looked at Gretel. There was a strange expression in his eyes. Like an animal cornered by a huntsman. Was he … scared?

"You weren't supposed to go near the witch's cottage," he repeated. "Gretel—"

"Don't blame this on Gretel!" cried Hansel. His spoon clattered against the side of his bowl.

"Hansel, calm yourself." Gretel placed her bowl on the table and rubbed her brother's shoulder. She felt sorry for him. Up until two weeks ago, her poor brother had believed everyone was his friend, and the land was a good place. "We should eat something."

"Eat!" Hansel gave a laugh that was almost a sob. "All I have done for two weeks is eat! How are you not angry, Gretel? He's our father, and he doesn't care." He shot Father a venomous look. "I attempted to protect you last night but I will not do so again. Albrect and the others won't let you get away this."

"I did not do anything!" cried Father. "Perhaps I had too much ale, but I remember—"

"All I remember is you willingly leading us into the trees," said Gretel, looking at Hansel. "You remember that too, don't you?"

Hansel nodded. "No one forced you." He paused. "Unless Ilse bullied you again."

The door banged open and in bustled Ilse. Father jumped, almost overturning his bowl. The timing was so exact that Gretel knew without a doubt that Ilse had been listening outside. So she was afraid, too.

Good. She should be.

A knock sounded as Gretel was scraping up the last of her porridge. Ilse opened the front door to admit Cristoph.

Wonderful, thought Gretel. She had been hoping not to run into him so soon, but it was no surprise he was here. Cristoph thought everybody's business was his own. Her betrothed took off his hat, giving Ilse his usual unnecessary little bow. He was three years older than Gretel, though could pass for more. Even as a child, he'd had one of those kinds of faces. Gretel could picture exactly what he would look like as an old man.

"Firstly, I am overjoyed that both Hansel and Gretel are home safely," he said in the stiff, courteous voice that always rubbed Gretel the wrong way. "Secondly, I am here to escort the twins to the inn. Lord Fabian wishes to speak to them."

Suddenly, the spoon in Gretel's hand felt impossibly heavy. She laid it down and drew a deep breath.

Hansel dropped behind Gretel and Cristoph on the short walk to the inn, perhaps to give them privacy – not that Gretel wanted any. She focused on attempting to warm her hands while not aggravating the burns. The sooner she got them seen to, the better.

"I searched for you every day, you know," Cristoph said. "The second we knew you were missing, I was in the forest."

Gretel made a non-committal noise. Cristoph ploughed on. "It was hard to know what to believe. Naturally, there were whispers that your father had abandoned you again, but he claimed you had decided to seek your fortune elsewhere. That felt believable." A pause. "Hurtful though it is. Is the agreement between us so very awful?"

And here he is, making it all about him, thought Gretel. She said nothing. The Green Gate was in sight now. She wished Cristoph would stop speaking. She needed to prepare herself, not massage his hurt pride. Everything depended on this meeting.

Cristoph's tone sharpened. "If you are hoping to deter me by maintaining a surly silence, it will not succeed. I hope when we are married you will not be this childish."

"I am maintaining a maidenly silence," murmured Gretel. "It is not becoming for a girl to speak out of turn."

Cristoph looked irked, even though she was parroting things the men of Westerleen believed. "I hope your conduct in front of his lordship is more respectful. I will wait downstairs while you are with him."

"Why stay? What Lord Fabian says to us is not your concern."

"Everything you do is my concern. We won't have any secrets when we are wed."

Their arrival at the inn spared her replying. The Green Gate would not be considered fine by an outsider, though it was grand by Westerleen standards, with not two but three floors. It was a rickety building that creaked in even the gentlest breeze. The smell of dust and ale was strong, as though it had seeped into the walls and floorboards. As a girl, Gretel remembered the walls being adorned by animal skins, but one by one those had vanished to be made into cloaks and blankets. The main room was saved from total dreariness by the cheering log fire.

Lord Fabian had, presumably, arrived by carriage sometime in the night. He had remained in Westerleen the first few days after Jakob had vanished, until business had forced him to return to his manor house a couple of hours' ride away. He and his son had only been in Westerleen in the first place as part of the progress he embarked upon each year through the villages that fell under his governance.

Gretel had only ever set foot inside the inn after dark. It had a different ambiance in the morning, and it felt wrong for her to be here now. Cristoph went to warm himself by the fireplace, shooting Gretel aggrieved looks she ignored. Hansel paced about and Gretel rocked backwards and forwards on her heels, unable to relax.

It is silly to feel on edge, she told herself. And yet she couldn't get Jakob's warning out of her head.

One of Lord Fabian's servants appeared at the foot of the

staircase and announced that his lordship would see the twins upstairs. Hansel hung back to allow Gretel to go first. The twins were led to the inn's best room. Lord Fabian was seated in a straight-backed chair by the fire, wearing a finely sewn tunic of deep, dark red. Unlike Westerleen men, he was clean-shaven and short-haired, his almost-black hair swept back from his face and only lightly peppered by grey.

Perched next to him on a stool was Jakob. Now that they were together, Gretel saw how much Jakob resembled his father. Gone were the filthy, ragged clothes and wild hair Gretel had become accustomed to in Esther's cottage. Clean and dressed grandly, with his dark eyes and sharp features, Jakob looked less like the boy she'd traded confidences with and a lot like someone who would dismiss her as an unimportant peasant. Someone distant, who inhabited a life she could only dream of. It suddenly seemed absurd she'd ever felt close to him.

Did she have this wrong? Gretel halted in the doorway, both intimidated and uncertain.

"Come, come, shut the draught out." Lord Fabian beckoned them forwards. Gretel shuffled in and bobbed a curtsey. Hansel joined her, and the servant closed the door.

"Are you both rested?" Jakob spoke up. "Today I feel like a

different person. A very alive person."

He winked. Gretel had the measure of Jakob's sense of humour by now but, even so, she winced. Lord Fabian gave his son a reproving look but did not comment.

"Last night's story has been relayed to me." The way he spoke was clear and crisp, a voice of precision and learning. Gretel knew from Jakob that Lord Fabian had received a full education at the far-off university in Levalliers City and had practised within law courts before unexpectedly inheriting the lordship. "I understand I owe you my heartfelt thanks for saving my son. For that, you will be for ever in my debt. You have my gratitude, and so does Westerleen. Your village shall have the assistance it needs.'

His voice was warmer now, and he was smiling – much more approachable. Gretel felt a smile nudge her own lips. She opened her mouth, then checked herself. *You are a girl of low rank. Let him speak.*

"You have also," Lord Fabian continued, "rid the land of a dangerous menace. Whether the witch was responsible for famine and poor weather as many in Westerleen believe, we will never know, but it's undeniable that she captured many boys over the years. I've spoken to bereaved families, from Westerleen and other villages, and well understand their devastation and loss. The witch is a monster. For that reason, it is proper and deserving that you receive a sizeable reward – the same as I would give a professional bounty hunter."

This time, Gretel was unable to prevent a wide smile. She had to stop herself shooting Jakob a triumphant look. She *had* judged this right.

"In the past, I have arranged for other such heroes to travel, or found them employment," said Lord Fabian. "However, based on the … ambiance of Westerleen at present, and your young age, I assume money would be of most benefit. Is that correct?"

Hansel shifted uneasily. In a gentler voice, Lord Fabian said, "You may speak. I wish only to help, Hansel."

And that was when Gretel realized.

The whole time, Lord Fabian had been addressing her brother and not her.

"Well?" asked his lordship.

Hansel looked Gretel's way. Surely, surely, he wasn't going to take full credit for this, as he had with the pebbles? Last night, she could excuse. They had been confused, and exhausted, and Gretel had felt too vulnerable to assert herself. But Lord Fabian could not be allowed to make the mistake the villagers had.

Jakob spoke before Gretel could.

"Father," he said. "You are making a mistake. Hansel did not kill the witch. Gretel did."

Lord Fabian frowned. "Mr Haufmann explained everything. I was under the impression the boy—"

"It wasn't me." Hansel's voice sounded thin. Horror crossed his face when he realized he'd interrupted. He stammered an apology, adding, "The story you were told is true. Everything about our escape, and the witch being flung into her own oven. But my sister is the one you should be thanking."

"I did tell you, Father," said Jakob mildly. "And you accuse me of never listening."

His lordship no longer looked so genial. It felt as though ice had settled across the room. Gretel had imagined this moment to be one where she felt good, but all she felt was a growing sense of unease. "I thought you had become confused. These stories are easily twisted when one is scared and tired, and the villagers said—"

"The villagers assumed," said Jakob. "I wonder why."

For the first time, Lord Fabian looked properly at Gretel. His eyes were hard and calculating. Lawyer's eyes. She could not help but take a step back. "So, this is true?"

"Yes." Gretel found her voice, but it was an effort to keep her tone measured and respectful. For the villagers to dismiss her was not a surprise, but for a lord, a man of learning and money, to ignore what she had done, from the lips of his own son... It was so disappointing. *Men are all the same,* said Esther's voice in her head. *Bullies or fools, the lot of them.*

"You pushed her into the oven?"

"The witch was about to kill my brother. I had to stop her."

"There is more, Father." In contrast to Lord Fabian's, Jakob's eyes were bright. He was enjoying needling his father, Gretel could tell. "It was Gretel who guided us back to Westerleen, picking a route that kept us safe from wolves and bears and who knows what else. Hansel and I were lucky she was there. We were both in too much of a state to have our wits about us."

If Gretel had been close enough, she would have kicked him. The more details that came out about Esther and her cottage, the more questions they raised.

Sure enough, Lord Fabian's eyes narrowed. "How did you manage to navigate the forest? I thought it was like a maze. We were unable to find the witch's cottage when we were hunting for Jakob."

Gretel had no choice but to lie, and hope it satisfied him. "While I cooked and cleaned for Esther, she told me some of her secrets. One was the route to Westerleen. And some say the cottage is magic, only revealing itself to children."

"Preposterous," said Lord Fabian. "Only narrow-minded peasants believe such things."

Gretel's cheeks flared. "I never said *I* believed it."

"That is irrelevant. What other 'secrets' did the witch share?"

"I didn't realize you had called Gretel here for an interrogation," said Jakob. "Hardly very grateful, treating your son's saviour like a criminal at the dock. I thought you had better manners, Father."

"Quiet. Answer, please."

Gretel realized she had stumbled on to shaky ground. Lord Fabian might be sceptical of Esther's powers, but that didn't mean he would hesitate to denounce Gretel if he thought she had in any way been the witch's accomplice. Meekly, Gretel said, "Only that it is true that she killed the missing boys, but that was obvious. There were bones everywhere. Human bones."

She drew a deep breath. And she was back, to the first time she had visited the cottage.

Prowling around the edges, misery and hunger heavy in her belly, but sharp enough to take everything in. Frail cobwebs hanging from windowsills, the filthy panes, the overgrown bushes and tangle of dead plants that must once have been a garden. If not for the warmth emanating from the house, Gretel might have thought it empty.

Oh. Her eyes widened. Gretel crouched down, brushing aside weeds and nettles. Propped in the earth were spindly yellowed sticks she had on first glance supposed were plant markers of some description. Closer, it was evident they were not painted wood. Far too irregular and curved and smooth-textured.

Bones. The sticks were human bones. Esther's victims.

Gretel had seen plenty of animal carcasses and never had they troubled her before, but coming face to face with human remains – of boys she had once known, boys loved and missed by their families…

Bile filled Gretel's mouth. She shot upwards, suddenly desperate to put distance between herself and the remains. Her back bumped into something solid that had not been there a moment ago. Gretel whirled round. Standing there, just as wizened and ugly and toothless as all the stories, was Esther. Grinning from ear to ear.

"My bones could have become part of Esther's macabre collection." Jakob's tone was pointed. Gretel shook herself. She had to stop slipping back into memories of Esther; that was done now, over. "Just think how inconvenient losing a son would be. One less person to arrange a grand marriage for."

Lord Fabian ignored his son, instead taking a sip of ale from his tankard. "Why did she do it? They were children. Harmless. Why only boys?"

"I don't know," said Gretel. "She was quite mad. Perhaps she did not have a reason."

"Does it matter, now that Esther is dead?" Jakob got up, crossing the room so he could stand beside Gretel, making his support clear.

Anger crossed Lord Fabian's face. "I will ask the questions, thank you," he snapped. "I agree with Albrect Haufmann that as soon as possible we should turn the witch's house upside down. We all deserve to know these 'secrets'. Wouldn't you agree?"

This last part was directed at Gretel, and she gave a little gasp. Was the lord … threatening her?

A cold feeling crept up her spine, and it wasn't the draught.

"I have matters to attend to." Lord Fabian had turned away. "You have my thanks."

"Gretel," added Jakob.

"Excuse me?"

"Her name is Gretel. You didn't use it, so I thought perhaps you had forgotten."

His lordship picked up a quill. "If you are not careful, Jakob, I will start regretting that you have been rescued at all."

"You have forgotten something else too." Jakob's voice was as sweet as Esther's gingerbread.

His father raised an eyebrow. "And that is?"

"The reward. A thank you is nice and good but, as you pointed out earlier, Esther was a monster. It's only fair that Gretel receives what you offered her brother."

Gretel stopped breathing. There was silence. Then Lord Fabian waved towards the door.

"You are dismissed, with thanks."

The fire inside Gretel blazed so viciously she was afraid she was going to scream, and keep screaming. She wasn't sure she could speak, or move.

If I were a boy, I would have received a life-changing reward. But I am not, and so I don't. I returned from the cottage ... to this?

From the small of her back, she felt light pressure. Jakob's hand. He'd known there would be no reward. He'd tried to warn her, but she hadn't listened.

He'd also put forward his own plan.

A plan that now was Gretel's only option.

Her breath caught in her throat.

Sure enough, Jakob said, "Father, there is something else I need to say. Before Gretel leaves."

"More?" said Lord Fabian archly. "I'd say you have said plenty already, Jakob. But then you always do."

"I learned from the best," said Jakob, so pleasantly that had she not been clenching her hands into fists Gretel might have laughed. "There is one part of the story the villagers do not know; one I thought you should hear first." He smiled at Gretel. "Do you agree?"

Gretel wished she had properly considered Jakob's idea back in the cottage. She'd hoped it wouldn't come to this, though in her heart of hearts she'd known it might be her last resort. Doubt raced through her head. Could she really trust him? Was depending on another person wise? Would this bring the freedom she craved, or was it just another trap?

"Gretel?" prompted Jakob.

She took a deep breath and nodded. Jakob turned back to his father.

"Gretel risked her life to rescue me," he said. "She kept my spirits up in the cottage. She has a generous spirit, and a bravery many lack. I knew perfectly well you would never reward her fairly, because to you she is irrelevant." His voice hardened. "Fairness matters to me, though. So, in exchange for my rescue, I made her a promise."

Lord Fabian stared at his son. His expression now gave little away – his legal training coming into effect, no doubt – but its stillness betrayed his absolute revulsion. "If this is a joke, it is in the poorest taste."

"It is not a joke." Jakob rested his hand on Gretel's shoulder. It felt awkward for him to be standing so close, but she stopped herself pulling away. "I promised Gretel that if I left the cottage alive, we would marry."

For a long moment, Lord Fabian's face remained as stone. Then he rose to his feet, brushing down his tunic in a mechanical sort of way.

"I wish to speak to my son alone," he said, his tone so calm that Gretel knew he was not calm at all. "Leave us."

Jakob gave Gretel's shoulder a reassuring squeeze before he stepped away. Gretel had for so long trusted no one but herself that leaving this to Jakob went against all her instincts. However, she knew insisting on staying would be a bad idea. So she followed Hansel into the corridor and the heavy door shut behind them.

Hansel cleared his throat. "We should wait downstairs."

We should listen in, thought Gretel. But the door was solid and thick, the room large. Even with her ear pressed to the wood, she doubted she would be able to hear much, especially as Lord Fabian did not seem the kind of man to shout, even in anger. And she did not want to worry Hansel further. Already he was looking bewildered.

Down in the main room, Cristoph turned from where he had been watching the fire. Hansel gave Gretel a reproachful look. She scowled back.

"Things went well, I trust?" Cristoph asked, with another of his infuriating little bows.

Gretel cut in before Hansel could speak. "Perfectly well, thank you."

"So what was said?" Cristoph sounded eager. *He is hoping we have been rewarded,* Gretel realized. *Of course he is. This is even better than Mother having money.*

She gave him a tight smile. "I prefer to keep that between myself and my brother."

Cristoph's eyes narrowed and for a second she thought he was going to rebuke her like a naughty child. Instead, he cleared his throat, as though about to commence a great speech. "Gretel, prior to … your disappearance, your stepmother and I had spoken. She feels it would benefit you to marry soon and I agree. You need guidance, someone to steer you in a way Ilse cannot." A note of petulance crept into his voice. "A lot of people would not tolerate you speaking to them as plainly as you do to me."

Shaken as Gretel was by what had been said upstairs, the interview had also left her feeling angry – and anger made her bold. "I have no desire for your guidance, Cristoph. You may soon find that a lot is going to change anyway." She paused, then added, "And you should know that it was I who killed the witch, not Hansel."

Cristoph started to laugh. Then he spotted Hansel nodding and stopped.

"This is true?" he stuttered.

"Completely." Hansel slid Gretel a look. "I am sorry I didn't correct everyone last night, Gretel. I was so relieved to be safe that I got carried away. I was going to put them right."

Gretel wasn't sure whether she believed him but that was not important. "They know now. Please could you leave, Cristoph? I wish to speak to Hansel alone."

Cristoph blinked. He was used to Gretel rolling her eyes and muttering under her breath, not asserting herself. She was a little taken aback herself. He started to speak, then clearly thought better of it. Instead, he picked up his cap from one of the tables, somehow managing to make the action come across as aggrieved.

"Whatever you wish, Gretel," he said, in a tone that rivalled

Lord Fabian for stiffness. He did not congratulate her or tell her she had done well. Did he feel threatened? Or simply not like the idea of so much attention being on her?

As soon as Cristoph was gone, Gretel faced her brother. There was a hurt expression in Hansel's blue eyes, so like her own.

"You and Jakob made a promise?" he said. "You never mentioned that to me."

We wouldn't have had to, if I'd been allowed to claim the reward that is rightfully mine, Gretel thought. "There was no time."

"It is genuine, then?"

"Why else would he say it?"

"To annoy his father? Anyone could tell there was tension between them. So, you had conversations in Esther's cottage? You became close?"

Gretel's pulse sped up. Hansel didn't sound suspicious, exactly. More … baffled. Had he really believed she had been cooking and cleaning for Esther the whole time? Carefully, she said, "He was captive, just like you. I brought him food and water, and tried to raise his spirits."

"You never mentioned that to me," he said again.

That wasn't all Gretel had chosen not to mention to her brother. If this conversation carried on longer, he would start asking even more awkward questions, and she would feel guiltier than she already did. "Hansel, all I was focused on was getting the three of us out of the cottage alive. Would it have made any difference for you to know Jakob and I talked to each other?"

Hansel still looked unconvinced. "I am surprised, that's all."

Gretel shifted her weight from one foot to the other, wondering how she could shut this conversation down. "I did save his life. He made me a promise."

"A promise does not mean much. He will renege on it before too long. These high-born folk do not care for us, not really. Aren't you being a bit naive?"

This was new. Hansel was never normally protective. Gretel had wished he would support her so many times over the years but, now that he was, she wasn't sure she liked it. "I don't have any reason to think Jakob would go back on his word."

"What about Cristoph?"

Cristoph, who could barely hide his disapproval of Gretel, and was only sticking around because he believed an old story about hidden gold. "He'll have no choice but to end our proposal if he is instructed to. Jakob outranks him." Unable to stop a sneer creeping into her voice, she added, "I doubt this will break his heart."

"That is unfair, Gretel. Cristoph has been patient with you."

"And that means I owe him my hand? Hansel, Jakob is a lord's son. What girl in Westerleen wouldn't be thrilled by such a promise? You could be more pleased. Lord Fabian said he was going to help the village, too."

After a moment, her brother smiled, though it didn't quite meet his eyes. "Let's hope he does. I just worry for you. When the gratitude of being rescued wears off, Jakob will have second thoughts. It's highly unusual, a lord's son being promised to a peasant girl. The stuff of fairy tales, even."

Gretel hadn't anticipated Hansel challenging her. She'd expected him to be delighted, to take everything at face value as he always did.

Perhaps she wasn't the only one the two weeks in Esther's cottage had changed.

"I do not need you to tell me something that obvious, Hansel," she said, smiling to show she was joking. "Maybe I am highly unusual, have you considered that yet?"

Hansel laughed, though it didn't sound very good-humoured. "Perhaps you will become so grand you'll pretend not to know us any more. I assume this promise means you will be leaving to live in the lord's manor. That is what happens with nobles, isn't it? Betrothed girls often stay with the boy's family before any wedding?"

"I think that's how it works. I have no plans of forgetting where I come from, if that is your concern."

"You will, though. Comfort and money turns people's natures."

"Who told you that?"

He shrugged. "It's something Father said once. It stuck in my head."

Maybe their father had been trying to justify how their mother's world had narrowed when she had married him. Gretel did not agree. Money was, rightly or wrongly, a gateway to opportunity.

Esther had taught her that much. Among many other things.

THEN

LORD FABIAN ARRIVES

Eight Days Before the Second Abandonment

The morning of Lord Fabian's arrival in Westerleen found Gretel pegging wet clothes on the line outside her cottage in the vain hope that somehow they would dry in the chilling breeze. She sang a lullaby her mother had taught her, more as a distraction from hunger than because it offered any comfort. She was almost done when little Brida Haufmann barrelled down the lane towards her, arms windmilling.

"The lord's carriage has been sighted!" she cried.

Gretel couldn't help but laugh. "Don't get so excited, Brida. He won't want to talk to you. And it is probably the same carriage as last year, which, if I remember rightly, was not nearly as grand as I was expecting."

"Maybe, but I still want a look. Come on." Brida clasped her hand. Her joy was so infectious that Gretel relented, tossing the final gown over the line and hurrying along to The Green Gate where a crowd was amassing. Many were children, skipping about and bouncing up and down as though they could barely contain themselves, but plenty of adults and teenagers were flocking along too, including men pausing their day's work. Their expressions were guarded and uncertain.

No doubt wondering if this visit will bring the aid Westerleen desperately needs, or be a false promise, Gretel thought. She was not superstitious or especially religious, but she found herself murmuring a little prayer under her breath. Surely Lord Fabian could not allow the situation to worsen? The elderly were leaning heavily on their sticks, propped up by their sons and daughters, as though too weak to stand. And they were the ones robust enough to leave their houses.

Minutes later came the whining and snorting of horses. A wooden carriage with shuttered windows trundled around the bend, flanked by four guards in navy blue uniforms, and came to a halt by the inn. Gretel squeezed to the front with Brida so she could get a better look. One of the guards opened the carriage door with a flourish to reveal a pair of boots with curiously pointed toes. Another murmur went round the crowd: a new fashion from the city. The man wearing the boots jumped out and stood with his back perfectly straight as he surveyed the crowds.

"Your lordship, welcome once more to Westerleen." Albrect Haufmann stepped forwards, executing a smart bow. Gretel wondered if he had been practising. Certainly, his hair and beard were neat and his jerkin was cleaner and less faded than the brown one she usually saw him wearing around the village.

Lord Fabian acknowledged him with a nod. "Mr Haufmann. I can see you received word of my visit."

"We did indeed." Albrect was taking care to properly enunciate every word and, unless Gretel was mistaken, soften his accent. "Let me show you inside. The famine is particularly bad this year I am afraid, but we can provide refreshment. The witch is to blame. She has cursed our crops again. And two boys have vanished from Westerleen this year already, and another from Winterbach. We badly need aid—"

Lord Fabian held up a hand, and Albrect stopped. "Let us speak of this in the warmth. Jakob?"

A boy of around Gretel's age clambered out of the carriage. If Gretel remembered correctly, his lordship had five sons. She guessed this must be the youngest. Jakob was unsmiling, though he looked sulky rather than stern.

Probably resents being pulled around dead-end villages instead of being free to enjoy his grand life, thought Gretel. From the way the boy clutched his fur-lined cloak to him, he resented the weather, too.

She wondered how Lord Fabian's son normally filled his days. No doubt plenty of study, with access to shelves upon shelves of books and swathes of interesting people who had seen the world and had stories to share. He would probably soon enrol at the far-off university, to be taught by the finest minds in the land. What must it feel like to step into Westerleen, where everyone knew each other and the closest there was to entertainment were card games or dice in the inn? Here, you could walk from one end of the village to the other in ten minutes, and see the same faces every time. Jakob probably looked down upon the place as backwards and unimportant. In fairness, Gretel couldn't blame him.

Lord Fabian and his son went into the inn. A few other men

followed. The door closed behind them.

"That is it?" asked Brida. She sounded disappointed.

Gretel patted her shoulder. "I expect so. Last year he toured the village once, then spent the rest of the time inside with your father and a few others."

Brida stroked her chin. "Maybe I can get Papa to tell me what they talk about later."

"I don't think your father would appreciate that. He already thinks you too headstrong."

"I like to know things."

That sounded familiar. "If you are that interested, eavesdropping is far more effective than asking to be told," said Gretel, and Brida laughed. She had a snorting kind of laugh, like a piglet, and Gretel liked it.

"You should be a teacher, Gretel," she teased. "I learn so much from you."

"No, you don't. I tell you nothing."

"Of course." Brida mimed shushing, then skipped off to join a couple of friends her own age. Gretel glanced at the door to The Green Gate. Last year she hadn't much cared what Lord Fabian and the men had discussed. Food had been abundant then, and home secure. But with the threat of imminent marriage – and the threat of being abandoned a second time – hanging over her, it felt important that she know what was said.

Gretel hesitated. Could she eavesdrop? The meeting room in the inn had thick walls, but they would leave at some point to walk around the village. Perhaps she could tag along somehow. It would be audacious, but what did she have to lose?

Albrect would be running through formalities with Lord Fabian and his sulky son for a while yet, so Gretel settled in for a wait. She perched on a barrel at first, but her toes and fingers began seizing up so instead she paced up and down the slim alley between the side of The Green Gate and the next cottage, hugging and rocking herself for warmth. One of the cats who kept the inn free of mice perched on a windowsill and watched her in a faintly accusatory way, before settling down on a tufty patch of grass to snooze.

When The Green Gate's side door did creak open, Gretel was in an almost trance-like state, and too slow to hide. Instead of Lord Fabian, Albrect and the other men, Jakob stood in the recess, cheeks flushed. His eyes fell on Gretel. She stared back, hoping she gave the appearance of someone who was supposed to be here.

"Can I help you?"

Jakob strode over, thrusting his hands into his pockets. "You could tell me where I can go in this place to enjoy myself. Surely there is more than the inn."

His arrogant tone made Gretel bristle. *Do not cause trouble.* And yet she could not quite hold her tongue. "What were you expecting? Shops, theatres, libraries? You have seen the extent of Westerleen already."

"That road is it?" Jakob flicked his head backwards.

"Apart from lanes leading to cottages, yes. If you wait, the boys your age will return in a couple of hours. Sometimes they wrestle or shoot bows."

"Not my idea of fun. Especially not in freezing temperatures. I don't know how you manage. I've never seen so much mud."

Gretel gritted her teeth. "We manage perfectly well. We are on high land and cannot help the cold."

"I pity you."

"I don't need your pity. A few Westerleen winters toughens anyone up."

"Well, does anyone play chess?"

Gretel shook her head, not willing to admit she only had the faintest idea what chess was.

"Darts? Checkers? Nothing beyond dice or cards?"

"This is a village and people have work to do. I am sorry if it doesn't meet your expectations."

"Rude," said Jakob, eyebrows shooting upwards.

"Speak for yourself," snapped Gretel. "Go for a walk if you are bored. See some more mud. Unless you are afraid of the cold, that is."

Jakob stared at her. Gretel stared back, unblinking. Then, the hint of a smile nudged his mouth. "If people are so busy working, why are you lurking out here?"

Annoyingly, Gretel felt the tops of her ears burning. "I do not have to explain myself to you."

"You *are* rude. You do know who I am, don't you?"

"I'm not the village idiot."

"No, I can see that." He laughed. For a moment, he did not look quite so sullen. Gretel released a slow breath, only just realizing how foolhardy she had been letting her temper get ahead of her. Antagonizing the lord's son? What had she been thinking? What if he complained to his father?

Fool. She cast her eyes downwards. "I apologize for my rudeness," she murmured. "Please do not judge Westerleen by my words."

Jakob waved a dismissive hand. "It doesn't matter. Show me

around. I assume you know the best places to walk. What's your name?"

Strolling around Westerleen alone with the lord's son would do nothing to enhance Gretel's already poor reputation. "It wouldn't be right for me to accompany you. If you want to walk, head to the end of the road, then turn left. You'll come to a river. It is peaceful there."

"As opposed to the forest, where the wicked witch I've been hearing so much about lurks? Tell me more about her. I cannot believe all those men are scared of a little old woman. They are acting that way to prey on my father's sympathy, surely?"

Gretel shook her head, already backing away. "Esther is dangerous."

"Why do boys go into the forest, then?"

"To hunt and chop wood. The boys go in groups, but it is easy to become separated."

"If she is such a monster then someone should do something about her."

"It is not that simple."

"Sounds simple to me." Jakob flicked a cobweb from his cloak. "It can't be that difficult to find your way through the forest. A few days' trek, perhaps. It would probably only take one brave villager to deal with her."

There was a lump in Gretel's throat, and for a second she was scared she was going to grab this boy by his fine collar and hurl him into the mud he'd sneered at. The way he dismissed their fear and pain, as though it was childish make-believe… He had no idea how people here suffered. If he had been the one who those dark, claw-like trees had closed around, knowing that his father was all but leaving him to starve…

Somehow, she swallowed the lump. "Sneer all you like. You don't know the forest, or the witch."

"If she even is one. I am not convinced real witches exist, or that her curses cause famine. She is probably only eccentric."

"I am sorry. I need to go."

He caught her arm as she walked past him. "Show me around, please. No one will care. They are all in the inn. Be as rude as you want. In fact, I encourage it. I like a good argument." He paused. "I don't mean to look down on your village. I am homesick, and tired of being forced to sit in dull meetings where my opinion counts for nothing. I used to have a lot more freedom than this—"

Yowl. Gretel jumped round. The sleeping cat was on its feet at the top of the alley, fur puffed up and swishing its tail. Was that the thud of footsteps? Had someone startled it – someone who'd been listening?

Gretel pulled her arm away from Jakob.

"Find your own entertainment," she hissed, and hurried away.

NOW

THE PROMISE

The Morning After the Return

After fifteen more minutes, Gretel could not endure waiting any longer. She'd started to pick at the blisters on her hands, and her flesh was hot and screaming.

"I need air," she announced, rising.

"All right," said Hansel. "We can stand outside then."

"No. I want to walk. And I would prefer to be alone."

"Aren't we supposed to be waiting for Lord Fabian?"

It wouldn't be Gretel his lordship wished to speak to. As she had just been reminded, her voice counted little. Outside the inn, the fresh breeze immediately cleared her head. Gretel laced up her cape. It was the colour of mud. Most villagers wore tones of brown, because dyed cloth was so expensive. *Mud everywhere,* thought Gretel. Jakob had been right about that. Westerleen looked drab this morning. Had it always been so colourless? Or was she seeing it with fresh eyes?

Esther had kept a wardrobe of colourful clothes. That had surprised Gretel until she remembered old Mistress Fischer's stories about Esther as a village girl, who, until she had turned to darkness, had been known to be particularly skilled with her needle.

"A bit of vanity never did a girl any harm," Esther had cackled when she caught Gretel looking. "A fine dress can fill a girl with power..."

Esther had permitted Gretel to wear her gowns. In them, Gretel had felt like a different person. Someone capable, someone stronger.

Gretel wished she'd thought to take some of the gowns with her when she'd fled the cottage. She turned towards the river. Normally, she would have been able to walk by without anyone glancing her way, but today it took an age because villagers kept running from their cottages to ask if the witch was really dead. They did not appear aware that she had done the deed; word had not yet spread.

By the time Gretel managed to escape from Westerleen, she was sweating again, and her head was buzzing. Further up, just past the bend in the lane, was a path descending to the riverbank, where sparse trees formed a little glade. Checking she was alone, Gretel hoisted up her skirts and clambered down, holding her free arm out for balance. Thanks to melting snow and then rain, the banks were close to bursting. Gretel didn't mind – the hush and movement of the water was soothing, even in its violence. Whatever happened in the village, nature lived on, vital and uncowed. Already she felt calmer.

By the river was a solid oak tree. Gretel slid her hand into an almost hidden groove within the trunk. Her fingers brushed cloth, and out came her old childhood quilt – cobwebbed and smelling of damp. Wrapped inside was a book. Gretel released a satisfied sigh.

Still here, she thought, and ran her palms over the familiar, worn, engraved lettering.

The Land of Amersren

"One day, I hope you'll be able to read this," Mother had said when she handed Hansel and Gretel the book years ago. "My mother gave it to me when I was little and made me promise that I would pass it on to my children. It's a lovely thing to have, even if all you can do is enjoy the pictures." She'd smiled, inclining her head to gaze across the fields. The warm sunlight had lit up the reddish sheen to her hair. "All the places inside could be adventures."

Hansel had soon tired of the book – staying still was never his strength – so it became Gretel's. The colourful pictures of far-flung cities and towns and mountains fired her imagination, especially when she grasped that it was not a story book and that these places were real. Mother, who had been taught basic letters as a child, passed that knowledge to Gretel, but only in secret. Gretel could not understand why – after all, Mr Weber taught some of the boys their letters in the cottage that passed for a schoolhouse. When she had asked about that, her mother had sighed.

"There are people who would disapprove, Gretel. Reading is a fine skill to have, and there is no reason why everyone should not acquire it, girl or boy, but here I would keep it to yourself."

After Mother's passing, Gretel had, with effort and guesswork, progressed from simple words to teaching herself to read fluently. It had been nowhere near as difficult as she had assumed and Gretel had relished the challenge. The thrill that danced through her when the marks on the pages all made sense was even now a sweet memory. Gretel could not imagine anything else giving her the joy that this book did.

Except perhaps one thing...

She closed her eyes and conjured up the illustration of Levalliers University that she had studied in the book so many times. It was several days' carriage ride away, but in her imagination, Gretel was there. Pale yellow brick, wide airy windows and tall turrets, circled by a moat – as impressive as the grandest of castles. Beyond the tall double-doors, Gretel imagined rich tapestries and chambers stacked with books and robed students keen to challenge themselves.

These students were not only male. According to the book, women, too, were allowed to study, providing they had a sponsor – a person of influence who could vouch for them and offer financial assistance. In her dreams, Gretel sat in the lecture halls – pen, ink and parchment in front of her – as a professor talked of literature and science and the other subjects she had only grazed in her learning and was determined to delve into further. The smell of ancient book dust hung in the air, sweet as perfumed flowers...

University. A stupid aspiration for a peasant girl, no matter how able. But then had not Mother always encouraged her to chase her dreams?

Almost no one knew of these dreams. Mother's warning about keeping her skills hidden had been sound advice. Unless they were cunning, all the clever women Gretel knew ended up being taunted or shunned or made to feel small. She herself had a hard enough time without giving the villagers another reason to mock her.

Esther had been clever, of course. Gretel had watched her totting up earnings in a leather-bound book after their one trip to the market. Her reading was not so strong, partly on account of her feeble eyesight. One night, quite early on in her stay, Gretel had been unable to watch Esther squinting at her own handwriting any longer.

"Let me read that."

Esther raised her thin eyebrows as Gretel drew out a stool and perched beside her. "Ah, yes, I forget you have an interest in books. Tell me, pray, how a girl like you has learned such things?"

Gretel scanned the page. It appeared to be a recipe – some kind of potion. Did Esther really have magic powers? "Mostly, I taught myself."

"How? Unless Westerleen has transformed from the sorry place I remember, they were not very keen on books, even for the chosen boys."

Gretel hesitated, but the urge to share with someone who might understand was overpowering. "I came to an agreement with a merchant. He traded animal hides, but had once been a teacher and was sympathetic to my desire to learn. Each fortnight he would lend me a book and then exchange it for another on his next visit."

"And what did he want in return?"

"Nothing." Gretel smiled, remembering. "He was lonely and enjoyed discussing the books. Some were about numbers, so I understand those, too. Once you grasp the fundamentals, they are not so hard." Mathematics was powerful, she had realized – emerging theories about what numbers could be used to do, from building to even understanding the stars in the sky, were staggering. "He said I reminded him of his daughter. I think she had died."

"Children perish all the time," Esther said dismissively. "The parent that gets too attached is a foolish one."

Parents perished all the time, too. What would Mother say if she could see Gretel now? Would she understand why Gretel was in the witch's cottage?

Gretel's gaze wandered to Esther's oven, and the screaming fire behind it. She pictured the merchant, with his lined, kindly face. Their arrangement – a sunbeam to Gretel in an otherwise grey world – had come to an abrupt end a few months ago with *his death. Gretel had surprised herself with how upset she felt. Not only because her source of knowledge was gone, but because she had become genuinely fond of the gentle, elderly man. In the end, they'd been friends.*

I am not cold and uncaring, as the horrible village boys make out, *she thought.* Maybe the problem is Westerleen, not me. I don't fit in there.

She didn't say any of this to Esther. Esther would only say it was a failing to become fond of anybody. It was one of her many rules.

"Don't trust anyone" had always been Gretel's.

And Esther would have done well to heed it...

"Gretel? Hello?"

She gave a start, almost dropping the book. Jakob was standing higher up on the bank, surveying the path down with a grimace. Gretel dived behind the tree, hastily wrapping up her book and stuffing it into the recess.

"Sorry," Jakob called. "I didn't mean to startle you. There really is mud everywhere, isn't there?"

Gretel stepped into the open. Jakob had just about managed to clamber down without losing his balance. His expression was a little wild, and his hair flopped over his forehead. It made him look less like his father, as did the smile he turned on her.

"I cannot describe how fine it feels to be able to walk where I want, rather than be confined in darkness," he said. "I will never take freedom for granted again. Are you hiding? The village is in quite the hubbub."

"It will be even worse when they hear I was the one who killed the witch." Gretel clasped her hands behind her back, taking a deep breath. "I didn't expect you to bring the promise up like that."

Jakob sidestepped to avoid one foot sinking into mud. "I didn't have a choice. Father was going to dismiss you with nothing. I told you that the only way you would get out of here would be through me. You did agree."

Gretel bit her lip. "We should have spoken beforehand…"

"How? Sneaking aside for a private word? My father hasn't let me out of his sight. If I hadn't said something then we'd have left Westerleen by now. Maybe I acted in haste, but we are allies, aren't we? He has no choice but to treat this seriously. A promise is a promise."

Gretel's frustration bubbled over. "But how can this promise ever work? A lord's son and a peasant girl? It is a ridiculous plan. And in case you had forgotten, I have been promised to someone else."

"The officious cretin who tried to listen in to your conversation with my father? One of our servants caught him at the door. You can't marry him. You'd be miserable."

"Thank you for telling me something I already know. It wasn't my choice."

"Which is why you need to leave." Jakob paused. "You still want to, I take it?"

Gretel let out an exasperated noise. "Of course I do. I didn't come back here to return to everything I hate. I couldn't bear that. I know that to you Esther's cottage was a prison, but to me it was a treasure trove of knowledge. A different life. To give that up…"

The rest of the sentence stuck in her throat. Jakob sighed. "I'm sorry, Gretel."

She wasn't sure exactly what he was apologizing for, but she was going to get nowhere by losing her temper. None of this was Jakob's fault. And she needed him. Gretel took a moment to breathe deeply. "I'm sorry too. So, what did your father say after we left?"

Jakob ran a hand through his hair. "It was … one of our livelier conversations. Apparently, you are an uneducated peasant who is so far beneath me as to be ignored, and I am impetuous and unruly. He is especially furious that the potential betrothals he and Mother were considering for me might come to nothing."

Anxiety tightened around Gretel. "I told you. It is a ridiculous plan. He will simply undo it."

"He will not." A touch of arrogance crept into Jakob's voice. "I said before, I won't be controlled by my father. I don't like conventions or rules. Having survived makes me all the more determined to challenge them."

"He could argue you weren't in your right mind when you made the promise. Or that I manipulated you somehow..." What else would Gretel do, were she Lord Fabian? Suddenly the answer was obvious. "He will attempt to pay for my silence," she gasped. "He knows we are poor and starving. And he won't offer the money to me."

The conversation would be held with her father. He who would agree on her behalf without a second thought.

Nothing would change.

This promise would be over before it had even begun.

"Then we'll stop him," Jakob said. "If you definitely want to go ahead with this?" Gretel hesitated and he went on. "If one of your concerns is being beholden to me, don't be. This suits me too, remember? I do not want to be betrothed to some far-off lady chosen by my parents who I've never met and probably wouldn't like."

"It's not only that. I don't fully trust you."

"I had to trust you, in the cottage. That didn't go badly, all things considered." He pointed to himself. "Still alive."

"Are you mocking me?"

"Of course not. None of this is amusing. If I stop to dwell on what nearly happened, then…"

"Then what?"

Jakob's eyes drifted along the rippling water. Then he shook himself and gave her another smile. "Never mind. Shall I give you my word I can be trusted? Will that help?" He paused. "I did think we were becoming friends."

Gretel rubbed her jaw. He was right. They had been. The return home was making her question everything. There was so much at stake – more so for her than Jakob. If things went wrong, he would be cushioned from the consequences by his rank and gender. She didn't have that security.

Being promised to him mightn't be so bad, she thought. *Who knows if any marriage will ever actually come to pass? In Lord Fabian's manor, there will be books, and tutors, and I will learn how to act in higher society. All things which might help me to enrol at the university.*

Gretel realized that Jakob was speaking. When she asked him to repeat himself, he said, "I asked how you were feeling about Esther. Murderous witch or not, taking a life cannot rest easy."

Gretel was trying hard not to feel anything at all. *Focus on the evil Esther did, and not the evenings we sat alongside each other discussing the ways of the world.* She had to believe she'd done the right thing. "I don't know. It does not yet feel real."

"You were so composed when you freed me from the cell. I could barely believe you had done it. Hansel was the one beside himself."

Her mouth twisted. "I should have let Hansel carry on pretending he'd killed the witch. It is the version of the story everyone would prefer."

"Not the true one, though."

But he did not know the true version. No one did. "You said you have a plan to stop your father?"

Jakob nodded. "We must swear a solemn declaration of promise to each other. Father will have no choice but to accept that. He is a stickler for tradition."

That wasn't enough. Gretel thought for a moment. "I have an idea." A twig cracked and Gretel froze, but when no other sound followed, she relaxed. "We must make an announcement, somewhere public, with many witnesses. There'll be quite a number of villagers who will object on Cristoph's behalf, but..." She glanced at him. "Your wishes trump his. Some may be hopeful that this will mean that your father will help Westerleen. Promises of this nature are regarded as binding when they are sworn." Oh, how relieved she was that her proposal to Cristoph had been less formal! "My father won't try to fight it if there are witnesses, even if he is offered money."

"Oh?"

Gretel pictured the guarded expression on her father's face this morning. He had surely guessed at the truth, or some of it. "Father is scared of what people think. They all know he abandoned Hansel and me again. The last thing he'll do is cause trouble."

Jakob regarded her in a way that made Gretel uncomfortable, as though he could see into her head. But he nodded and pushed off the tree he had been leaning against, dusting himself down. "Shall we go and make a spectacle of ourselves then?"

More being stared at. Gretel pushed aside her nerves. "It is market day, so that is where we should go. The inn this evening would be better, but I don't think we can wait that long."

"Agreed." Sounding apologetic, Jakob said, "Might I suggest

that I do the talking? I know this is your home, but the more I say, the fewer murmurings there will be that this is against my will. Also, I won't be challenged."

Gretel nodded, hating that he was right. "I will stand there and look demure."

Jakob lodged his boot on a drier part of the bank and scrambled up. He held out his hand for Gretel. She stared at it a moment, then she shook her head and swung up herself. Together they returned to Westerleen.

The market was heaving, the buzz palpable. For the first time in ages, people were animated, even though there was little to buy. Gretel had been so focused on herself that she had not given the villagers much thought. For the first time, she realized that as well as disposing of the witch, she had given them something else. Hope. For the first time in years, no one needed to be afraid.

"Here she is!" Mistress Meier spotted Gretel first. She smiled warmly, and curtseyed to Jakob. The other women followed suit, a wave of bobbing heads. Would they curtsey to Gretel when they heard of the promise? She felt conscious of everything in a way she hadn't last night – her worn gown, the way she walked.

As a chattering crowd thronged around them, Jakob held up his hand. "Please, may we have a moment's quiet?"

The authority with which he spoke made him sound exactly like Lord Fabian. Where was he at the moment? Hopefully not with Gretel's father, who at this time was normally in the trees with the other woodsmen. Over the top of capped and coiffed heads, Gretel caught sight of someone familiar: Ilse.

"I am indebted to Gretel." Jakob's voice was steady and strong. "Simple thanks are not enough. For that reason, I wish to, here, now, with all of you to witness, make her a solemn promise as thanks. A promise that, in time, we will marry. And that I swear."

Gasps flew through the crowd. Carefully avoiding her burns, Jakob took Gretel's hand and kissed the air above her knuckles. Gretel braced herself for the reaction. *How could you? What about Cristoph? You betray us.*

Yet every single face was shining with joy and wonder. And the chatter erupting around her...

Congratulations. *They're congratulating me. They're happy.* Gretel heard herself thanking them – but felt as though she was watching from far away. This was just like one of her mother's fairy stories. Not her life.

"Gre-tel! This is wonderful!" It was Brida, who had squeezed her way to the front and was now jumping and clapping. "I knew you deserved something special! Don't forget me."

"Never," Gretel said. She sought the crowd for Ilse, but either she had gone home, or was hidden by the jostling bodies.

A couple of Lord Fabian's servants were in the crowd too. *There is no way he can deny the promise now, not with so many witnesses,* she thought. Jakob had used solemn, binding words.

Gretel felt a smile break out on to her face. Despite her doubts, despite what had happened with Esther, hope swelled inside her. So much for the grim future she had been afraid of, the one foretold to her just two weeks ago...

"Your greatest fears will come to pass, every single one of them. All that awaits you is misery. You will never leave Westerleen. I see a man you do not care for, who will be bound to you for ever. A disappointed woman, whose bitterness drives her to cruelty. A boy, who will enjoy everything you crave. Any joy is fleeting. Hardship beckons – unless you can fight your fate. But then you will lose something even more valuable."

Not any more.

Hopefully, no one would ever find out how Gretel had tried to fight fate – and what she had been prepared to sacrifice.

THEN

JAKOB IS MISSING

Seven Days Before the Second Abandonment

Someone was shaking her. Gretel murmured, tugging her blanket tighter around her shoulders. Her dreams had been fragments of the day before – rushing to see Lord Fabian's carriage, skulking about outside The Green Gate, the conversation with Jakob. But in her dream, everything had taken on a nightmarish tint … culminating in her being ejected from the village.

"No, stop, I have nothing," she murmured, but the shaking only intensified. Her eyes, foggy with sleep, blinked open. Through the gloom she made out her brother's face. *The last time I was woken in the night, we were taken into the forest.* Suddenly completely awake, she shot into a sitting position.

"It's all right," Hansel said quickly. "Don't worry. It isn't … that."

Gretel let out a long breath. For a moment, she had been catapulted back in time, so vividly she could smell wet earth and mossy air. "Then, what…"

"The lord's son is missing. Someone thumped on our door a few minutes ago. I am going out to help search."

Gretel went still. "What do you mean, missing? There *is* nowhere to go missing in Westerleen. Unless…" She thought of the forest. "If he wanted to walk, he should have…"

Gone in the direction I told him. She checked herself. Something warned her not to admit she had even spoken to Jakob.

Hansel spread his hands. "I don't suppose you can think of anywhere he might have gone? I know you have places you like to disappear to."

So that was why he had woken her. It wasn't, realized Gretel, the early hours as she had first supposed. The dusky light peeping through the shutters indicated it was first light, close to the usual hour woodcutters rose.

Gretel hadn't thought Hansel paid her enough attention to have noticed she disappeared sometimes. She considered the question, then shook her head. "Nowhere that a boy who set foot in Westerleen only yesterday would find."

"I hope he hasn't gone into the forest," muttered Hansel as he looped a belt around his tunic. He did not need to speak the word – *Esther.*

Gretel hugged her knees to her chest after Hansel left, worried despite herself. Surely Jakob would not have been arrogant enough to venture somewhere so dangerous alone? He knew Esther existed. Yet he'd mocked the threat she posed.

Why doesn't someone do something about her? Those had been his words. Had Jakob decided that someone could be him? He didn't seem the kind of boy who'd endanger himself to play hero, but he had been bored, and seemed to have some kind of point to prove to his father. Perhaps he had decided to see if the fearsome witch was so fearsome after all…

No, Gretel decided. He could not be that stupid. Far more likely, Jakob had wandered off and become lost. Slipped over in the mud he'd been so scathing about and broken an ankle, perhaps. It would serve him right.

Gretel rose and went about her day, which was more

interesting than usual because something novel was happening. Girls Gretel rarely had much to do with stopped to chat, guessing where Jakob had gone. But by sunset there was still no sign of him. Westerleen had been combed, the roads scoured miles in every direction, enquiries made at the closest villages. Woodsmen had spread through the edges of the forest and found nothing.

Gretel stood watching as the hunt continued under the light of flaming torches, her cloak drawn tightly around her shoulders. There was a familiar sinking feeling in her belly. A couple of times a year, this exact scene played out. A missing boy. A fruitless search. Everyone knew how this would end.

Should she find Albrect, or even Lord Fabian, and tell them what Jakob had said yesterday? Would it help? No. Everyone knew he had to have gone into the forest by now – there was nowhere else. All it would achieve was trouble for her.

So Gretel turned her back and headed home. *I have no reason to feel guilty. It was his decision, and his decision only, to brave the forest.* And yet she did feel guilty. She could have explained why Esther was such a threat, persuaded him into understanding, introduced him to Hansel and his friends. No one deserved such a terrible fate.

"Gretel." A hand settled on her arm. Gretel let out a yelp, but it was only Cristoph. Face lit by a flaming torch, he looked ghoulish.

"You should not have startled me like that." She rubbed her arm, feeling funny. Cristoph had touched it almost exactly the same place as Jakob had yesterday.

"Well, you should not be creeping around after dark."

"I do not creep," Gretel had not meant to snap, but she was shaken. "It is natural to be curious."

"Is curiosity all it is?"

Cristoph's words were loaded, in the kind of way a parent addressed a child who had erred and lied about it. Gretel did not know how to answer, so she tried to walk away.

He caught her arm again. "I saw the two of you talking yesterday."

Gretel went limp. Of all the people to catch her with Jakob! "We exchanged a few words. He asked me if there was any entertainment because he was bored."

Cristoph made a harrumphing noise, like a grumpy horse. "Why were you lurking around outside the inn when you should have been busy at home? Were you hoping to bump into him?"

"Of course not."

"I don't believe you. Shall I share what I think, Gretel? You believe yourself to be destined for better things than life here. That is why you give yourself airs and graces that would deter a less reasonable man than I."

Was he being serious? Of course he was: Cristoph didn't joke. Despite herself, Gretel was a little afraid. She had never seen him riled like this. "You are being absurd. *He* spoke to *me*."

"I am not a bad match, you know." Cristoph barely seemed to have heard. "I am hard-working and honest and dutiful, but no, you want grander things than I or anyone else here can provide. Ilse warned me your mother turned your head with her stories of life outside the village. She was correct. You are headstrong, and difficult, and do not know your place. You need to be subdued."

"Subdued?" Her voice shook. "How exactly do you intend to subdue me, Cristoph? With force?"

"Of course not. I would never lay a finger on you. I don't approve of men who mistreat their wives."

"How fortunate I am!" cried Gretel, fear making her unguarded.

Cristoph's expression tightened. "If you were not so unruly, you would be more content. You could belong, enjoy having friends who aren't eight years old. Brida will tire of you before too long."

She stepped away. "Leave me alone, Cristoph. I do not want your advice."

"You need help, Gretel." Cristoph's voice rose too. "I've seen you sneaking about when you should be working. Sometimes you are missing for hours. What is so fascinating about the river? You know it is dangerous there when a current is up."

Gretel had started to walk away but this stopped her. "You have been following me?" she whispered.

He folded his arms. "I watch you sometimes, to check you are safe. There is no need to sound so outraged."

Two teenage sisters scurried past, swinging baskets. Gretel caught a snatch of their chatter, something about a warm winter blanket finally being finished. *That is a normal conversation,* she thought, dazed. *Unlike whatever* this *is…* There was no regret or shame on Cristoph's face, only righteous belief.

"I thought I was alone," she hissed. "How dare you?"

"We are betrothed. There should be no secrets between man and wife." He paused. "Though I am starting to think we shouldn't marry. Our agreement was never a formal one."

Gretel thought she might be sick. If Cristoph walked away, Ilse would promise her to Heinrich Mulch. She'd seen the old man earlier, bent double, coughing phlegm into his sleeve.

"No. Please don't say that."

"Why not? You clearly don't want me. There is nothing stopping me from calling off our agreement."

Suddenly Gretel's fight was gone, and all she wanted was to run far, far away. So she did just that, pelting up the track towards home, because in the darkness she had nowhere else. This time Cristoph let her go. *I cannot live this life, I simply cannot.* Her parents had been in love. Even her father and Ilse had married because they wanted to. Gretel had always assumed she would at least *like* the person she wed.

Perhaps, Gretel vainly tried to convince herself, *perhaps she could change.* Fool everyone into thinking she was no longer "difficult". Cristoph might calm down if she apologized. He at least was young and healthy. Life together might not be terrible, if she bit her tongue every time she spoke to him.

But then I would be playing a part, for ever. Living a lie. And who wants that?

Cristoph would never support her reading or travelling. She would be stuck. Especially if later they had children, the thought of which made her even sicker. She would be forced to watch her brother do everything she could not… Hansel, who didn't even care about seeing anything beyond his village. He had no idea how lucky he was. None of those boys did.

Back home, Gretel crept into the bedroom and pummelled her pillow, venting all her anger and fear, before falling into a sleep plagued by nightmares – nightmares that had every probability of coming true.

NOW

A FAMILIAR FACE

The Morning After the Return

The market erupted into celebration. Gretel found herself buffeted between well-wishers. All over, people were cheering her name. Children danced. Women she hardly knew kissed her stinging hands. They urged her to use the influence she would gain to help them.

"Please." Gretel tried to project her voice above the cheering. "This is too much. Of course I will not forget Westerleen. I could not, even if I tried."

Abruptly the cheering died and was replaced by silence. A ripple passed through the crowd as heads swivelled, then bodies moved to clear a path. Gretel saw why. Standing by one of the stalls was Lord Fabian, flanked by two guards. His face was expressionless.

"As you were." His voice was cold. "I would hate for this news to detain you any longer."

Reluctantly, women picked up their baskets and led their children away.

A seamstress leaned to whisper in Gretel's ear. "We will hold a proper celebration later. We need some joy to hold on to."

She squeezed Gretel's hand, right over the sores, and Gretel snatched it away. Jakob stepped beside her. His hair had become even more dishevelled and his cheeks were flushed.

Lord Fabian swept his eyes over the pair of them. The only hint of anger was a vein pulsing in his forehead.

"I suppose you think what you have just done is clever," he said, quietly enough that only they could hear.

"You suppose correctly," said Jakob, then stopped as Gretel shook her head. It would benefit neither of them to anger Lord Fabian further.

Lord Fabian jerked his head then turned and walked away,

clearly expecting to be followed. Gretel started after him then stopped so abruptly she almost tripped. The merchant at the closest stall was staring at her, with shrewd, calculating eyes. The man was small and middle-aged, with a bald head and a sparse brown beard. The cloth trader, who often visited Westerleen. He had no reason to gaze at her so oddly…

Then Gretel knew. A chill ran up her spine.

This man had seen her out with Esther. That day, at the market.

"What's the matter?" Jakob asked.

Gretel began walking again. "Nothing. I saw someone I did not expect to see, that's all. Come. We need to go with your father."

Back inside The Green Gate, Lord Fabian barked at Gretel to remain in the main room while he spoke to Jakob. Gretel counted to fifty, then crept upstairs. She was fully expecting one of the guards to be standing sentry but the corridor was empty. Gretel squatted at the door to the room Lord Fabian had occupied earlier, pressing her ear to the keyhole.

"… absolutely preposterous." That was Lord Fabian. "Have you any idea just how foolish that was?"

"I have every idea how foolish you think that was." Jakob spoke more quietly than his father but Gretel could hear clearly enough.

They must be close to the door. She tensed, primed to sprint away if she needed to.

"This is the most wrong-headed thing you have ever done. You will regret it. If this is another attempt to express your anger at the situation with Ottillie..."

Ottillie was Jakob's sister. Gretel knew exactly which situation Lord Fabian was referring to. Jakob started to object, but his father spoke over him. "No, don't answer or I really will lose my temper. I thought better of you. I assume this is another childish attempt at rebellion, one of your tiresome little games. What will the peasant girl do when you grow bored of this? Have you considered that?"

Gretel stiffened.

"Am I permitted to speak?" Jakob sounded equally cold now. "You asked so many questions and yet you commanded me to be silent, which anyone would agree is counter-productive..."

A thud answered, so loud that Gretel leaped back. Had Lord Fabian knocked over a chair? In a second, Gretel sensed someone would storm out. She fled. Downstairs she sank down staring into the fire's flames, as though they somehow held the answers.

Little games. Was there something Jakob hadn't told her? He had called them allies. They had a mutually beneficial agreement.

He genuinely seemed to want to help. Yet Lord Fabian had hinted otherwise…

Maybe she wasn't the only one keeping secrets.

Ten minutes later she was summoned upstairs. Lord Fabian stood by the window. Gretel dropped her best curtsy. She did not make eye contact with Jakob, sitting behind the table covered by his lordship's papers.

"You have created quite the stir," Lord Fabian remarked.

Gretel distrusted his mild tone. She said nothing. Jakob's father raised his eyebrows – or at least she thought he did. With the window behind him, it was difficult to read his expression in the unlit room.

"I assume you believe that we will be obliged to take you with us when we return home. You think coming to live in my house will be a gateway to a better life, I suppose?"

"I assume nothing, your lordship."

Lord Fabian sighed, rubbing a hand over his face. It was uncalloused, with smooth skin. A hand that wielded a quill, not an axe. "I have your best interests at heart, even if you cannot see that. Making this foolish declaration… It will bring no good for either of you."

He spoke as though he was prophesying, and Gretel shivered.

All that awaits you is misery.

"However," Lord Fabian continued. "I recognize I cannot undo the promise my son has made you, bone-headed though it is." He looked at Gretel. "I wonder, Gretel, if you and I might speak alone, as it appears I have no choice but accept your continued presence?"

"Of course," said Gretel, at the very same time Jakob said, "No."

There was a pause, then Gretel tossed him a pointed look.

"Sons should respect their fathers," she said.

Reluctantly, Jakob left. The door clicked behind him. Gretel wetted her lips. This man's decisions would affect the course her life took from now on.

Lord Fabian paced from one wall to the other. Then he swivelled to face her.

"Had the little scene in the marketplace not happened, I would have spoken to your father. If wealth is what you seek, you would have had it."

No, Father would have. Gretel remained silent.

"Now I have no choice but to take you in. Do not be mistaken – no one in my household will welcome a peasant girl trumping the natural way of things, however overjoyed the villagers here are.

You would do better to stay where you belong." He paused. "I will ensure that your basic needs are met, but that is all. While in my house, you will not touch my son and you will be chaperoned at all times. If you are planning on manipulating your way into his heart, you will be thwarted. Not that I believe Jakob ever intends for any marriage to ever take place. I won't hear of arrangements being made for several years." Another pause, a significant one. "Although I do not expect you will remain with us for that long."

Was that a threat? Gretel took a step backwards.

"Do you understand?" his lordship's tone was glacial now.

She managed a nod.

Men are bullies or fools, the lot of them, Esther had claimed. Gretel knew which his lordship was now.

THEN

FORTUNE TELLING

Six Days Before the Second Abandonment

The night passed without any sign of Jakob. *Definitely taken by Esther,* thought Gretel. She strolled through the village mid-morning, listening to the chatter. As she neared The Green Gate, the door flew open. Lord Fabian stormed out, expression thunderous.

"How can you have searched everywhere?"

"I trust my friends and neighbours, your lordship," Albrect

followed, a tightness to his face that told Gretel he was working hard to contain anger. "We've covered the tracks, the cottages, the river and the edges of the forest. It is too big to comb completely."

"Look again, then! Show my men exactly where this wretched witch lives. They could not find her cottage yesterday."

"The witch's cottage only reveals itself to children."

"Westerleen really is an uncivilized backwater if you allow yourself to believe such impossibilities," Lord Fabian snarled. "This witch needs to be slain if she is such a monster, the sooner the better. There are plenty of bounty hunters who would gladly do so. I would summon them if I believed they would get here quickly enough. Do you enjoy cowering in fear and losing your sons? Search harder!"

Gretel's breath caught, but Albrect did not put Lord Fabian in his place. Gretel was not sure if she respected his self-control or not. Albrect muttered something that sounded like "as you wish", and marched off, calling for yet another search party. The ball of anxiety Gretel had woken up with inside her belly tightened. They wouldn't find Jakob. He was probably already dead. What did that mean for Westerleen? His lordship would never send aid now.

Winter stretched long and hard ahead of them. Where would Gretel and everyone else be by the time fresh green leaves spouted from trees, and the flowers teased their way to bud? Would they even survive?

Hours passed. Men and boys trickled back into the village without news, exhaustion etched all over their faces. The mood at home was equally despondent. Gretel found it hard to concentrate on somehow preparing a meal from two turnips, a greening potato and the remains of a rabbit carcass. Her father sat at the table, resting his chin on his hands. When Ilse asked him if he planned to visit The Green Gate that night, he shook his head.

"All I am good for is sleep. I'll not step near the inn while Lord Fabian is in such a dark mood."

"What a surprise." Ilse rolled her eyes. "He blames us rather than his son's stupidity."

For once, Gretel agreed with Ilse. Hansel spoke up. "Lord Fabian should blame the witch. It is her spells that ruin harvests."

"His lordship dismisses Esther's dark magic," said Father. "I think he even doubts she takes the boys. He says the children run away for a better life."

"Maybe Lord Fabian will summon the bounty hunters," said Gretel.

Her father's brow furrowed. "Bounty hunters?"

"It was only something I overheard."

Ilse laughed. "Bounty hunters would be precious little use against Esther, grand weapons or not. It is hardly possible to slay a monster you cannot find."

"Little Emich Fischer wants to be a bounty hunter," said Hansel. "He's been fascinated ever since the storyteller at the last spring festival spoke of them. Do you remember? He spoke of the man who disposed of the river creatures near Ennisport? Killing monsters and being rewarded richly sounds like a fine and exciting life, Emich says."

Neither Father nor Ilse responded. They never found Hansel's stories about what the village children said or did interesting. Gretel slopped the stew into wooden bowls, adding the last of the well water to make it go further. Her father sniffed at his meal as she set it in front of him.

"What is this, Gretel?"

"The best I could do," muttered Gretel, drawing out her chair. "I thought it better to save the carrots and second potato for tomorrow."

"God have mercy on us," muttered her father.

"Well, I am grateful to have any dinner at all." Hansel gave her a smile. "And this is hot – just what we need. Thank you, Gretel."

Gretel returned the smile as she sat.

The family ate in silence, the only sound slurping and clinking when spoons were laid down. Hansel's leg was jiggling under the table. *Nervous,* Gretel thought. Little wonder. The twins had heard *God have mercy on us* before, three years ago...

The winter they'd been led into the forest, and not expected to return.

Gretel leaned close enough for Hansel's hair to tickle her nose.

"It won't happen again," she whispered. "Try not to worry."

"It is all right for you," muttered Hansel. "You will be protected. They will simply wed you to Cristoph early."

His tone made it clear he thought that a good outcome. Gretel swallowed. "If we are worried, we can tell Albrect and the others."

"They won't care; not now. They have their own families to protect and feed. They are probably even expecting us to vanish. Things are worse than they were before."

Gretel pushed her bowl over to Hansel so he could smear the last dribbles of stew with his finger and wrapped her arms around herself. She wished she could reassure him – and herself – but Hansel was right. Everyone knew that history so often repeated itself.

Only this time, they would be entirely alone.

*

Gretel awoke to yet another joyless day of surviving. After she and Ilse had completed the usual chores – preparing as filling a breakfast as they could, fetching fresh water from the well, making sure her father and Hansel had everything they needed for the day ahead – Ilse announced that Cristoph's mother was coming to the house.

"It is time we began to prepare for your wedding, Gretel," she said, with a falsely bright smile. "I have put aside an old dress of mine we might alter."

A knock at the door announced the arrival of Leonetta, Cristoph's mother. Gretel brewed tea, then changed into the dress and stood mutely as Ilse and Leonetta inspected her.

"You mentioned the spring festival before, Leonetta, but sooner would be better, I think," said Ilse. "Everything could be prepared in a month or so. Would that be agreeable to your family?"

Leonetta considered this, then nodded. "I will speak to Cristoph."

"Perfect. What do you think, Gretel?" Ilse shot Gretel a sly look.

Gretel shrugged. Leonetta frowned.

"Most girls look forward to their wedding day," she said sharply. "My son will make a fine husband. You are lucky to have him."

"Yes, Gretel," said Ilse. "You could do a lot worse."

She might as well have said the words Heinrich Mulch. Gretel shifted from one foot to the other. It felt as though she was struggling to breathe.

"I'm sorry," she muttered.

"Cristoph is the one you should apologize to," said Leonetta. "He told me you had a disagreement. I assume you do not want him to have second thoughts."

Gretel took a deep breath. Dully, she said, "Of course not. I'll apologize."

Leonetta's expression softened. "It is natural to be nervous. By the time the wedding day comes, you will feel differently."

Gretel changed back into her ordinary clothes and sat and listened to the two women discussing plans, a forced smile on her face. As soon as Cristoph's mother left and Ilse's back was turned, she slipped outside and took huge gulps of air. Then she ran, putting as much distance between herself and home as she could.

Gretel only stopped when her legs started to hurt. She leaned against a tree, pushing hair off her hot face.

If only she could escape before the wedding – or after it. Cristoph's family traded animal hides. On rare occasions when they had an abundance to sell, they journeyed past Lord Fabian's manor to towns further west. Perhaps she could request to be taken too and disappear…

But then what would she do? Without money, she would be alone on the streets. No one would help her – no one with good intentions, anyway. And those towns weren't much better than Westerleen, just larger.

It is a daydream, just like Mother's gold.

Jakob had been right. There was nothing here other than mud. Gretel realized she had wandered up near Westerleen's draughty church, its graveyard besieged by tenacious weeds. Leaning against the crumbling wall a little further along were Brida and her friends, examining each other's palms.

"… your love line is crooked," Brida was saying. "That means a rocky marriage, perhaps more than one. Or even a secret lover!" Her friend giggled, nervous but excited. At least they had found a way to take joy from this morning. "And here we have your life line. It trails off halfway across your palm…"

"What does that mean? Do I get ill?" The little girl sounded worried. Brida hesitated, then gave her friend's pigtails a playful tug.

"I don't know. I am not a real fortune teller, Enneleyn. If you really want to know what awaits, have your fortune read when a teller next comes to the village."

Clever Brida, to turn the conversation around and reassure her friend. Gretel felt a faint pang inside. It felt a lifetime ago she had been Brida's age, free to enjoy games without worrying about survival. Not that she had ever had friends the way Brida had. The other girls complained she was serious and awkward. Maybe they were just parroting what they had heard, or maybe they simply didn't like her. Gretel couldn't tell.

Brida's group were still playing fortunes, though by now their predictions had got wilder and less plausible. Fortune tellers did come to Westerleen, often around the time of the spring festival. From everything Gretel had seen, their predictions had been accurate. Anna Weber had married Thadeus Koch, even though he had not been the most handsome or prosperous man vying for her hand. The Fischer child had been a boy. And disaster really had befallen the Neydeckers when a tree crashed across their roof in a storm.

Perhaps if Gretel had her fortune told, there would be a pleasant surprise. Something to hint at joy around the corner; that she wasn't trapped. But the spring festival might as well be a million years away – and by then she would be married.

Fortune tellers are not the only ones who can tell the future. Esther the witch has powers of foresight, doesn't she?

What if I knew?

The thought slid into Gretel's head and lodged itself there like one of the weeds in the graveyard. It followed her on her walk, and back into the cottage and even to bed, as she lay awake yet again. It ate her up as the days trickled by, a thirst that could not be quenched however many times she told herself no.

What if I knew? And she *could* know … if she was brave enough. Seeking Esther out was dangerous, reckless and stupid. There were a hundred reasons not to. Like being captured and killed. However dark things looked, Gretel was not that desperate. She told herself she would find another way to challenge fate – one that did not involve the witch.

If only she could figure out what…

NOW

CONFRONTING ILSE

The Morning After the Return

The moment Gretel left the inn, villagers surrounded her, bubbling with further congratulations and asking her to describe the moment she had pushed the witch into the oven. So now they knew. Hansel must have told them. Gretel had always yearned to be seen but, now that she was, it felt all wrong. She was no hero. She pushed past, saying she was tired and needed to rest. She wanted to go somewhere quiet, somewhere to think, but she knew she should go home. Ilse would know by now that Gretel had killed Esther. And Ilse had been at the market. She might even have noticed the way that merchant had been staring. If anyone was going to unpick Gretel's story, it would be Ilse.

Her stepmother would never keep quiet, not if she could cause trouble. When had she become such a twisted, malicious bully? Before Mother's death, Gretel remembered Ilse as quick-witted and funny. It had been a great treat for Gretel to be allowed to accompany the two of them to market or listen to their chatter as they sat podding peas or peeling apples.

All was still when Gretel pushed open the door to the cottage. Suspiciously still, even. Her skin goose-pimpled. She abruptly became aware just how badly her hands were stinging. She would bathe them in ice water. Her head was beginning to throb, too.

Then a chair scraped. Gretel whirled round. Ilse stepped forwards, out of a shadowy corner.

"You had to be selfish, didn't you?" Her voice shook. "We could have been rich, if only you had allowed Lord Fabian to speak to your father. This promise benefits no one but yourself. *Selfish.*"

Gretel unlaced her cloak. Strong. She had to be strong. The

merest hint of weakness and Ilse would seize upon it. "You would know. You persuaded your husband to abandon his children. Not once, but twice."

"I did not. Anyone who says so is lying."

"I heard you three years ago, Ilse. I know it was you."

"I learned my lesson. I am not stupid enough to make the same mistake twice." Ilse came close, standing just inches in front of Gretel – close enough that Gretel could smell the woodsmoke on her clothes and see the spark in her eyes. They had sparred often, but there was something different about her this time. Something more dangerous. "All I said to your father is that I was concerned about the winter. His decision to lead you into the forest again was his and his only."

"Everyone knows you want Hansel and I gone."

"I had nothing to do with this."

Gretel wished she had gone somewhere else. She still felt shaken from seeing Lord Fabian. "If I were you, Ilse, I would be scared. Abandoning children is frowned upon. I don't think Father will be the one the villagers blame, do you?"

"I was here, at home, asleep, and knew nothing of it. That is the truth."

"Your truth, maybe. Your card is marked, and you know it.

Once untrustworthy, always untrustworthy. People forgive, but they do not forget."

Ilse tossed her head, as though all that was immaterial. Gretel pressed on. "People already talk about you. I've heard plenty of murmurings that you only married Father because of Mother's money..."

Her stepmother half-smiled. "Dear me, Gretel. I thought your brother was the dramatic one. What an outrageous claim."

"It is true, isn't it?"

"Tell me," Ilse said sweetly. "How did you get the lord's son so smitten with you, Gretel? Did the witch help? Did you use a spell or potion, perhaps?"

Gretel forced herself to remain calm. "I don't know what you mean."

"People will soon realize there is more to this than meets the eye. The lord's son would never look twice at a sullen peasant girl who isn't even pretty, grateful for his life or not." She stepped forward. "You seem shaken. Have I hit a nerve?" Ilse paused, but Gretel did not trust herself to speak. She could already feel her cheeks had coloured. "I could see you as a witch, Gretel. Perhaps Esther shared much more than you have let on..."

Gretel's heart thumped hard. Then the door swung open and

both Gretel and Ilse jumped, the charged atmosphere snapping. Ilse accidentally swept her palm over the table and a knife clattered to the floor.

Gretel's father shuffled in, eyes on his feet. With him were Albrect and several other men. They entered, filling the room. Albrect removed his hat and cleared his throat.

"I think you know what this is about."

For a split second, Gretel thought he knew everything. But Albrect's eyes were on Ilse. Gretel released a shaky breath and reached out to hold on to the back of the chair for support. She spotted Hansel at the back, biting his lip, his hands deep in his pockets.

Ilse bobbed her head and curtseyed. The perfect picture of a mild-mannered housewife. Yet, for the first time, Gretel thought she looked vulnerable. "May I offer you herb tea?" Ilse asked.

"Tea will not be necessary." Albrect looked a little unsettled, perhaps thrown by the gracious reception. "Hansel came to speak to us, and your husband has now admitted everything. What you forced him to do for a second time, Ilse, was unacceptable."

Gretel's eyes flew to her father, but he had turned away. Ilse flinched, but held Albrect's gaze. "I did not force Georg to do anything. I am not the one who makes the decisions. I regret what happened three years ago, and when I swore it would not happen again, I meant it."

"That is not what your husband says. At first, he claimed the twins requested to be led into the forest. Then, when we refused to believe that, he broke down and admitted the truth. That he took them there. When we asked if you had pressured him, he didn't deny it."

"This is slander." Ilse's voice had started to shake. "I may, yes, have voiced *concerns* to Georg. That is all. The twins are my dear friend Mathilde's children and I promised to look after them."

That didn't stop you last time, thought Gretel. Ilse's act was convincing. The very picture of the wronged woman. She held her breath. Would Ilse be believed?

"Hansel tells a different story." Albrect appeared unmoved. "He claims you dislike your stepchildren, and clash often. Especially," Albrect's eyes flickered Gretel's way, "with your stepdaughter."

His tone invited comment, but Gretel shuffled further towards the shadows. She sensed the less she said, the better.

"Strong personalities always clash," Ilse said harshly. "Do you have an amicable relationship with all of your children, Albrect? I hear little Brida is quite the handful."

"We are not talking about my family." Albrect didn't like that,

Gretel could tell. "So you concede you have a strong personality? A strong personality that you could use to pressure your husband into abandoning his children?"

Ilse stared at the men. The colour began to drain from her face. *She has realized the trap she is in,* Gretel thought. "So, you are all lawyers now? This is nonsense. When I discovered what my husband had done, I was stunned."

Another man spoke up. "No father would abandon his flesh and blood by choice. We know Georg has struggled over the years. He admitted earlier that he is weak and cannot think clearly when pressured."

"So weakness absolves him?" demanded Ilse. "Why am I not afforded the same understanding and forgiveness? Life is not easy for me, either."

Ludwig Neydecker jabbed a finger towards Ilse. "That is true. Life is not easy for you. The home is your domain. You are the one who cooks and feeds everyone, who knows about the difficulties of obtaining food. You knew how desperate things were. It stands to reason you would persuade Georg."

Gretel winced. How could they believe such shaky reasoning? Ilse was gaping now, looking wildly around for support.

"Georg," she cried. "This is wrong. You know it is."

"Sorry, Ilse," mumbled Father. "You did say we would be better off without the twins."

"That did not mean I wished them to be lost in the forest!"

"You knew Father would take it that way, though," said Hansel. "I am fed up with you telling him what to do all the time. He's not been the same since you came into our lives. Father and I used to be close. I looked up to him…" He blinked, eyes glassy, then, with sudden spirit, added, "And you are wrong to be so mean to Gretel and chastise me for being simple."

Ilse ignored Hansel. She faced Albrect. "I did not do this."

Albrect shook his head. "It really would be best to stop arguing."

Ilse went silent. Then, the defiance in her eyes faded. *Defeated*, thought Gretel. She was surprised to find her hands were trembling. What an ugly scene to witness!

"What happens, then?" Ilse's voice was a whisper. "Am I to be punished?"

"That is to be discussed," said Albrect. "I do not think your neighbours will take kindly to the news." He smiled at Hansel. "Thank you for coming to us. I know you are loyal and it cannot be easy to talk about your family with outsiders."

Hansel glowered. He looked surly and stubborn – words

usually used to describe Gretel. The men closed together, voices dropping as they spoke between themselves. Gretel's father sunk into the closest chair and stared at his boots.

"May I say something?" asked Ilse. She held up a hand as Albrect started to object. "I am not going to argue. I can see that is impossible. But I think it only fair that I raise a few other things you might like to investigate, seeing as you are so keen on discovering the truth." She tossed a smile Gretel's way, one that dripped malice. "Are you really going to take the story of Gretel slaying the witch at face value?"

Albrect frowned. "Hansel told us, and the lord's son corroborated the story. Why would we not believe them?"

"Don't you think it is odd that Hansel remembers so little of his capture? He is a strong lad. He had a bow and knife. Esther was old and half blind. Surely he would have put up a fight?"

Gretel knew silence was no longer an option. "When the witch's cottage appeared we were tired, hungry and thirsty. Hansel ate some gingerbread that was outside. Esther must have drugged it. Jakob will tell you the same thing."

"I wouldn't put too much stock in what the lord's son claims," said Ilse. "I am not the only one questioning their promise." She glanced at Ludwig. "Your wife was at the market. She remarked on how strange it was that Jakob should want Gretel too. The witch didn't imprison Gretel, did she? Perhaps one of the secrets Esther shared with Gretel was how to bewitch people."

"Gretel would never be in league with the witch!" cried Hansel. He went over to Gretel, looping his arm around her shoulders. "I won't let you say such things. Don't worry, Gretel, no one will believe her."

Gretel leaned into Hansel gratefully. She had never heard him sound so passionate before.

Ilse merely arched an eyebrow. "Didn't you mention discovering a nasty wound on your shoulder, Hansel, when you came to? I don't see why the witch would have hurt you, if you were already drugged."

Gretel silently cursed Ilse and her eye for detail. Hansel's injury was all but healed. Ilse must have spotted his torn jerkin and asked about it. "We were attacked by a bear," she said. "I don't know if you remember that, Hansel, but you were injured."

Hansel frowned, thinking. "My memories are hazy," he admitted. "But if you say so, Gretel, I'm sure it must be true."

"This is the first we have heard of a bear," said Ludwig.

"It did not seem an important detail."

"I wonder, Gretel, if there are other details you have chosen to omit?" said Ilse, and Gretel's mouth went dry. "Like why you remained in the witch's cottage? You said yourself that you weren't imprisoned. You had plenty of opportunities to escape. Yet you chose not to..."

Hansel leaped in. "Gretel stayed because she wanted to save me and Jakob."

"Really, Hansel?" said Ilse. "I know you are dim at the best of times, but you cannot believe that, surely. Gretel barely tolerates you."

"That's not true." Hansel squeezed Gretel's shoulders, and Gretel felt a lump form in her throat.

Ilse faced Gretel. "I noticed a merchant staring at you earlier. He confirms you were in Eastown with the witch just days ago." She paused. "He said you looked friendly. Close, even – like grandmother and granddaughter. Chatting, smiling, helping her lift things, fetching her a drink... Hardly the way I would expect a Westerleen girl to act around a murderous witch."

"I had to keep on her good side." Gretel's voice was hoarse and sounded horribly unconvincing. The men were all silent now, watching.

"Did you have an arrangement with Esther, Gretel? Perhaps when the cottage is searched, we will know the truth of that. As I said before, I can see you making an excellent witch..."

"Gretel killed Esther," cried Hansel. His hands were balled into fists, face flushed. "I saw it happen. If they were friendly, why would she do that?"

"Good question," Ilse said. "Perhaps something happened."

"All that happened was the witch decided to eat me, and Gretel had to stop her," said Hansel. "She was always pretending to get along with the witch. Weren't you, Gretel?"

"So, Gretel is good at pretending? Interesting. Some might say pretending is one step away from lying." Ilse's smile was wide now. "Perhaps *all* of this is a pretence."

Silence stretched. Gretel could not think what to say. Then Albrect stomped forward and grasped Ilse's arm.

"We will hear no more poisonous words. Gretel killed the witch and deserves respect."

Ilse shook herself free. She crossed the room, pausing in front of Gretel. "Well done on enacting your revenge upon me, stepdaughter. I applaud you. You've been clever. But, as I think you know, I can be clever too." She leaned forwards, her voice brimming with anger. "I am going to get to the bottom of your lies. And then I will enjoy *my* revenge."

THEN

THE FOREST AGAIN

The Evening Before the Second Abandonment

Gretel lingered on the track her father took home from The Green Gate. It had been several days since the conversation with Cristoph, where he had mentioned her being subdued, and since she had witnessed Brida and her friends telling fortunes. Leonetta had visited again earlier. Cristoph's family were happy for the wedding to be moved forward. A date had been set: a month from today.

Gretel had barely slept. She had spent the hours since Leonetta's visit agonizing over what to do.

I have no choice, I have to escape, and I cannot delay, she kept repeating to herself, but each time she thought she knew her mind, doubts resurfaced. Her head felt heavy as though she was trapped in a deathly nightmare, but it was real, real, real.

Going into the forest was madness. Many had perished there, seeking out a fabled new life. And yet – what choice did Gretel have? Things were desperate enough, surely. She had to take control of her own fate.

She thought of the wild animals that roamed the trees and were bold at night. But she would have Hansel and his bow with her, she thought. She would need to make sure of that.

Before too long, Gretel's father appeared, his worn brown jerkin and breeches blending into the mud and trees. He frowned when he saw her. Gretel took a deep breath and blew it out slowly.

"Is there something wrong?" her father asked, as Gretel fell into step beside him.

Was she really going to do this?

All that awaits you is misery.

Yes, she was.

"We are struggling, aren't we?" she said.

Father sighed. "Everyone is struggling. We will get through it."

"Will we?"

She let the question hang. Her father rubbed at his eyes. He always looked tired now, and ale made it worse. Did he lay awake worrying? Or was he simply getting old?

"Let us not talk of this, Gretel."

"I'm not a child, Father. I know everyone was hoping that Lord Fabian would help us. That won't happen now, will it? It's been six days since his son vanished. And we all know what that..."

Means. She could not say it. Unexpected bile had flooded her mouth at the thought of Jakob. Father kicked a branch off the path. He didn't appear to have noticed her discomfort. Gretel used the lapse to pull herself together. *Focus.*

"I do not know what you expect me to say, Gretel. I cannot reassure you, so what is the point in talking about it?"

"There is a solution though. Isn't there?"

Father stopped, for the first time making eye contact. "You will be married soon, Gretel. Worrying about you will be Cristoph's responsibility."

"I don't want to marry him, Father, and he doesn't want to marry me either. Even less do I want to be promised to someone like Heinrich Mulch. You don't want me to be unhappy, do you?"

"What is this other solution, then?"

It wasn't easy – she felt sure he must be suspicious – but Gretel pinned his gaze. "Do not pretend you haven't thought about it. I am sure Ilse has."

"That is not happening a second time."

He hadn't denied anything. That told her all she needed to know.

"Maybe your friends will judge you less harshly this time. Maybe…" She paused. *Courage, Gretel.* "Hansel and I are older now, and more robust. Better able to negotiate the peril of the forest. I know Ilse believes it might be better if we were gone. Maybe you do, too."

A crease appeared on her father's weathered face. "It does not matter what I think. Gretel, I cannot endure the ire from our neighbours once again. Life was unbearable before. Only now do the men look at me with anything other than disgust. It was wrong."

"People wouldn't blame *you*, Father. Everyone knows how much Ilse hates us. They will assume she manipulated and bullied you. She was the one at fault three years ago. It was her idea – I know it was. I overheard you talking."

She waited for him to contradict her, to acknowledge his part. He didn't. Gretel felt a twinge of disgust.

She slipped her hand into his, the way she had as a child. His skin was hard, a scar from an old accident creating a groove in the palm, and he smelled of the inn. "I don't want to stay here and starve," she said quietly. "That would be worse than anything. Before you bring up my wedding again, who knows if we will even survive a month? If it came to a choice... I would rather take my chances in the forest. Especially when there is a full moon. It would be in Hansel's best interest too, even if he cannot see it."

Her father glanced upwards. The moon sat low in the sky and cast soft light over the track. His eyes watered.

"I will take care of Hansel for you," she said.

Still he did not answer. He was thinking about it, she could tell. She could not apply too much pressure. Her father had to believe this was his decision. Gretel racked her brains, then knew what she needed to say.

"I think Mother would want us to have a chance," she whispered. "I fear we will not have one remaining here."

Father gulped, and that was when she knew he would do it.

"You are late." Gretel and her father jumped. Ilse stood a few paces away. Neither had noticed her approach. "Why are you here, Gretel?"

146

"Leave her be, Ilse," said Father. "She was keeping me company."

Gretel blinked, unused to him defending her. Ilse narrowed her eyes.

"Is that so?"

She sounded disbelieving. It was funny seeing Ilse in light of the conversation Gretel had just had. *Oh, Ilse, you have no idea the trouble awaiting you when he lets you take the blame for this.*

"I don't know why you are smiling, Gretel," snapped Ilse.

Had she been smiling? Gretel quickly relaxed her face. "Your eyes were deceiving you," she said smartly, and went into the house. Her heart was thumping, but in a good way. Despite the weakness of hunger, she felt alive. Maybe she had got this wrong, and Father wouldn't do it. But if he did – and she thought he would – the real question was when. Perhaps it would even be that very night…

"Gretel."

There was a weight on her shoulder. A hand. For a moment, Gretel thought she was dreaming. She shifted on to her side, rubbing her eyes.

"Hansel? Are you all right?" she mumbled.

The voice that rumbled out of the darkness was her father's. "Get dressed and come downstairs, Gretel. Quietly, please."

Gretel sat up. Her skin prickled as she drew in a deep breath. *It is happening again,* she thought. *And I am ready.*

Downstairs a knapsack and a single pouch of water lay on the table. A candle burned low, flickering dull light on Father's face. He wore his trekking boots. The twins' cloaks were slung over the back of a chair. Outside it was dark. Gretel guessed they had been asleep for a couple of hours.

The dead of night. A perfect time to vanish.

Gretel felt Hansel step close. She glanced over, and he stared back with dead eyes. He looked lost, suddenly twelve years old again. He hadn't uttered a single word. He already knew what this meant.

Father took a swig from his own water pouch, which Gretel suspected contained something stronger. Even though she had expected to be woken tonight, disappointment mingled with the anticipation and fear inside her. He hadn't put up any fight at all.

"Twins." Their father sounded choked. "I didn't want to do this but I now see that we have no choice. I hoped, we all hoped, that Lord Fabian's visit would bring aid to Westerleen, but it looks set not to be. You must leave and find a life elsewhere."

"No," whispered Hansel. "I want to stay here with you. Father …
you cannot do this to us again."

Father shook his head. His eyes were bloodshot. He took another
swig. *To work up the courage to be a coward,* thought Gretel. His
voice sounded detached, as though he had put anything he had ever
felt for the twins in a box and sealed it tightly. "I am sorry."

Hansel stumbled on to his knees. He clasped his hands together,
as though in prayer. "Please, Father. Another day. Just one. I'll find
food – something—"

"Gretel." A note of panic sprung into Father's voice. He was
losing his nerve, she realized. Quickly she joined her brother and
placed a comforting hand on his shoulder.

"It's for the best, Hansel. A day will make no difference to
Father's decision."

"No, Gretel!" cried Hansel. "This is our home. The forest –
Esther – if we go into it – one way or another, we'll die!"

Her brother burst into tears, sobbing like a child. "Come on,
Hansel." Gretel crouched down, taking his shoulders. "We need to go."

They walked into the forest in silence. Gretel fought to keep calm
but, as the branches closed around them, memories she had hoped
never to revisit emerged from the darkest recesses of her mind.

It felt darker than last time, as though there was less air. And deadly cold. It made her a little dizzy, and she kept glancing over her shoulder. Father swayed as he walked. Beside her, Hansel was still sniffling. He held his bow limply and kept tripping over branches and roots. Gretel hoped he snapped out of this soon. She hadn't heard any snarls or howls – and the forest animals hadn't preyed on her the last time she had gone deep into the forest, the previous morning – but that didn't mean they weren't there ... and it was night-time now. She was relying on Hansel to protect them both.

The moon shone full and bright. Gretel searched the forest floor and found what she was looking for, glowing in the moonlight. *Good,* she thought, and murmured a silent prayer of thanks.

Her father was veering to the left. "Father, not that way," she called. "Come, closer to me."

"Why?" He sounded belligerent. "You know the forest better than I do?"

"Of course not, but if you are going to leave us, don't we have the right to choose our own path?"

Father mumbled something. How aware was he of what was going on? That pouch must be empty by now, and he had spent the evening at the inn. He was making so much noise crashing about. Surely the forest animals would hear. Gretel's lower back was dampening with sweat. This was far more chaotic than she'd imagined.

She smacked her brother's arm. "Hansel. Wake up! You can't fall apart now. If there are wolves or bears about, they will hear us for sure. Be alert."

"Being mauled by an animal or starving in a bush, what's the difference?"

Gretel gritted her teeth. "Please, Hansel. I need you."

Hansel shook his head, but he did at least thread an arrow into his bow. Ahead of them, Father was beginning to wheeze.

"This is as far as I'll go," he said, stopping. "I wish you all the luck."

With that, he stumbled away without a backward glance. In this state, Gretel wasn't sure he'd even find his way safely home, but she couldn't worry about him. What would the villagers think when it dawned on them that the twins were gone? Probably that they'd been abandoned. It was the obvious conclusion. Not that she would ever return to Westerleen to find out.

Already Gretel's teeth were chattering. She grasped her brother's shoulder, guiding him forwards.

"Come on. The best thing we can do is keep moving."

"Where to? There is nowhere, Gretel. We don't have food this time, and barely any water. Ilse didn't even bother to wake up! How long has she been whispering to Father about abandoning us again? Did you not notice? You're the one who is in the house all of the time."

Gretel did not reply, concentrating on walking in the right direction. Hansel carried on, "Father promised. I thought he cared... Gretel! Are you even listening? How can you be so cool-headed about this?"

"Hansel, shush. You are being too loud. This way."

"Why does it matter which way we go? We are doomed. Unless Albrect and the others notice we are gone, and come to find us..."

Let him cling on to hope, Gretel thought, if that made it easier. *Not that there is any, not for him.* A sudden memory from years ago crystalized: she and Hansel tucked snugly together in the big bed, listening to Mother's stories. This one had been funny, and their giggles had been loud enough to disturb the birds outside.

Gretel swallowed. She had to think of the future, not the past, or else her resolve would ebb away.

They fell into silence, Hansel following Gretel as she navigated deeper into the trees, stopping several times to be sure she was going the right way. She'd thought he might become suspicious but he simply followed, shoulders slumped as though the fight had left him. Snow drifted downwards, settling across the twigs, brambles and dead leaves that covered the forest path. Her toes turned to ice in her boots, and her fingers were now so chilled she could barely move them.

Not long now, she thought, as faint sunlight teased its way through the bare branches. *If we can only keep going...*

Thump.

Gretel shot round. Eyes shone through the brambles behind them.

"Hansel!" she cried, the same moment that a large creature broke from the bush, teeth bared and snarling.

NOW

SAYING GOODBYE TO WESTERLEEN

Two Days After the Return

The next day, Gretel prepared to leave Westerleen with Lord Fabian and Jakob. Lord Fabian had no reason to linger and would be returning to his manor. Gretel did not need long to gather her few belongings. *Not much to show for a life*, she thought, gazing at the small knapsack. She had never lamented her lack of possessions, or really questioned it before, but what she had looked suddenly drab and unimpressive.

Esther's cottage had been full of all kinds of interesting things, and she imagined Lord Fabian's manor would be too.

It was just about light enough so Gretel stole outside and headed to the riverbank. Her book was where it should be, though one edge had become soggy – she hadn't been able to wrap it properly in the quilt yesterday. Gretel ran her now bandaged hands over the parchment. Strange to feel so melancholy on the day when she would sit in a carriage for the first time ever, and finally see more of the world outside Westerleen. Perhaps in the months that came she might even travel to the places depicted on the book's pages. She would miss it. The book had been a constant companion in times when life was darkest.

Soft footsteps sounded behind her, followed by an exclamation. Brida tumbled down the bank, grabbing a branch to steady herself.

"I didn't realize it was so steep," she cried. "Ouch. I came as soon as I could."

"Thank you," said Gretel. She had managed to pass a message to Brida last night. "I know it is early but I mightn't get a chance for a proper goodbye."

Brida wrapped her arms around Gretel and gave her a squeeze. "This is partly because I am freezing but mostly because I really will miss you," she said. Her tangled hair had water droplets in it and smelled of pine. "I know I have my own big sisters but they are not as fun as you are." She glanced up. "I think you are incredible, Gretel. I thought you were strong before, the way you never did anything you didn't like, but I doubly think that now. Do you know what I like best of all?"

When was the last time someone had hugged her like this? Gretel was more moved than she would admit. "No. What?"

"That *you* were the one who saved everyone. Not Hansel. Not the lord's son. You."

If only it was that simple. Gretel glanced at her feet.

Brida carried on. "I can imagine you in the house, waiting and watching for an opportunity to kill the witch and save everyone. Finding your way home is really something too. Once you get in deep, the forest is a maze, my father says."

Gretel knew she needed to speak but she couldn't. Why was it that she was able to tell half-truths and even outright lies to everyone else but hesitated when it came to an eight-year-old? How could she say *I am not any kind of hero, not really.* How could she ruin something that had so inspired her friend? This story might change Brida's life. Change other girls' lives. Make them realize they could be more. The idea was humbling, and Gretel felt rather small.

"I had better get back soon," she muttered. "How are things at home?'

"Father says I am cheeky and I suppose I am. Mother tells me not to take it to heart; that he has a short temper sometimes because he spends all day worrying about other people's families."

"Maybe he will relax now he knows no more boys will go missing. Now, I want to give you something," Gretel said, gently pulling back. She felt Brida's eyes on her as she went to the tree and withdrew the cloaked book.

"Oh," breathed Brida. "This is why you sneak away?"

Gretel handed her the book. "Take a look. It used to be my mother's. It shows all the places beyond Westerleen."

"But I can't read."

Gretel could have taught Brida letters and a few simple words if she had thought to. Pass Mother's legacy on. Now there was no time.

"You can look at the pictures," she said. "They're inspiring."

"Maybe one day, when you're a grand lady, you can summon me to be your servant, and then you can teach me to read?" Brida suggested.

Gretel half-smiled. "Maybe."

"My parents say that when they mean no. It was just a thought.

You don't have to. Do you like him, then? The lord's son? I liked the way he bowed down to you at the market. And he has nicer teeth than Cristoph."

At that, Gretel laughed. "He has a sense of humour Cristoph lacks, that is for sure."

"Do you really want to give me your mother's book, Gretel?" Brida turned serious. "Don't you want it yourself? I'm sure you could take it with you."

Gretel hesitated, torn. But she shook her head. "It was a comfort to me and now I want it to be a comfort to you. That's what my mother would want. I have plenty to remember her by. In here." She tapped the side of her head.

"What about Hansel?"

Hansel.

Last night, she had been under the covers, almost asleep, when her brother's voice had come through the darkness.

"Gretel? Do you think they were wrong?"

Gretel had groaned and forced her eyes open. "What?"

"Albrect and the others. They were so sure Ilse persuaded Father to abandon us. And so was I, but…"

Gretel had sat up, now completely awake. "How can you be doubting her guilt?"

"She denied it so vehemently. She really fought them, Gretel. Maybe she was telling the truth?"

"Of course she wasn't." Gretel's voice had come out sounding harsher than she'd intended. "You think Father is lying?"

"There is something he is holding back. I can tell. I felt sorry for Ilse, the way they surrounded her."

"That is the stupidest thing I have ever heard you say. Ilse wouldn't feel sorry for you if you had been in her position. Go to sleep, Hansel."

Her brother hadn't spoken after that, and the next morning he had been suspiciously quiet. What was going on in his head? Gretel hoped he wasn't about to do anything really foolish.

After showing Brida the nook in the tree, and the best way to wrap the book, the two girls headed back to Westerleen. A few women were drifting around the streets, waving off men and boys hurrying to begin work in the forest or the field. They deliberately turned their backs on Ilse, who was further up the track by one of the cottages. She was speaking to Hansel. Gretel frowned. Her brother was often out at this time – he hated being cooped inside, even when he had no work to do – but it was unusual to see Ilse this early anywhere but home.

Gretel was unable to make out Ilse's expression, but she

appeared to be doing most of the talking. Hansel shifted his weight from foot to foot, shaking his head. His expression was a mix of uncomfortable and apologetic. Gretel wondered what they were talking about.

She did not get a chance to find out. Cristoph emerged from a side track. Gretel contemplated ducking behind a house or a barrel – but no, it was too late, he'd seen her.

Perhaps I owe him a conversation, she thought, before correcting herself. *No, I owe him nothing. But if a few words will ease my leaving – for both of us – I can spare him a moment.*

"Carry on," Gretel murmured to Brida. Brida pulled a face but did as she said. Gretel waited. Sure enough, Cristoph joined her.

"Gretel." His manner was even stiffer than usual.

"Cristoph," she replied. "I am sorry if what happened yesterday caused you pain. That was not my intention."

"What happened yesterday, as you delicately put it, is that a boy who has no business meddling made you a solemn promise and, because he is of high rank, his wishes trump mine. The agreement we had is over, without my consent."

Gretel tried a smile, but it felt wrong. "Cristoph, let us be honest. Our betrothal was testing us both. With me gone, I am sure you will find someone you like better. It is a good thing."

"You would say that. You are leaving, and heading to a life of riches." He stepped closer, and Gretel backed away. Something stirred in his usually steady eyes: jealousy? "If the lord's son was one of the village boys, I would take him somewhere and make him regret this. People are laughing at me. Did you know that? Poor, silly Cristoph, discarded like an apple core, or potato peel, to rot."

Gretel was fast coming to the opinion that all men were dramatic. "Again, I am sorry you feel that way, but people will forget."

"I will not forget. You have made me look a fool. Remember, I saw the two of you, outside the inn. I wonder now if you were plotting."

Even though that conversation had been completely innocent, Gretel still felt a stab of panic. Had the doubts Ilse had voiced about her spread? Were others now also thinking that something did not add up? "Why would the lord's son plot with me?"

"I don't know, but there is no way a rich, educated boy like him would want to marry a peasant girl, not even if she saved his life. Like goes with like. Something is not right. I know more than you think, Gretel."

"What do you mean?"

Cristoph gave a short laugh. "That's rattled you, has it?" Gretel cursed herself. *Too hasty, too keen.* "All right. I will tell you. I know that six days after the lord's son disappeared, and shortly before you also vanished, you were in the forest all day."

He had been watching her. A chill settled on Gretel. "I wasn't."

"You are lying. I didn't see you return myself, but some of the boys did. They said your gown was filthy. More so than it would be from a day spent wandering through the trees. And you were not carrying anything, which is curious, because when you first went into the trees, you had some kind of bundle in your arms."

Gretel couldn't deny it. She knew she'd been seen returning to Westerleen, by Hansel and his friends. So they'd talked. And Cristoph had noticed the bundle she'd been carrying, though he could have no idea what was inside.

She had to get away. "I care not what you think. Goodbye."

She stepped around him and walked on. It was only with supreme effort that she did not look back. Another enemy. Another threat. Another person asking awkward questions.

Cristoph was not as sharp as Ilse, but he still worried her because, unlike Ilse, he was liked ... and a man. That made him credible. She hoped fiercely that Cristoph's hurt pride faded once she was gone. That he was just talking big to make her feel small.

But still, she worried.

THEN

THE GINGERBREAD COTTAGE

*The Morning of the Second Abandonment
and Two Weeks Before the Return*

A bear. Its bloodthirsty snarl as it charged sent Gretel's heart into her mouth. Hansel's arrow flew hopelessly wide. Then it was upon them.

Hansel just had time to snatch the knife from his belt and push Gretel backwards before it bowled him to the ground. All was spittle and claws and teeth and blood. Gretel couldn't tell whose.

The knife went flying. Gretel dived for the blade but lost her footing. Brambles tore into her skirts as she rolled on to her back, then pulled herself to her feet. Something bellowed in pain. The bear, or Hansel? If this all went wrong because of a dumb animal ...

Mist swirled around her ankles. Suddenly, the air was sweet. And then the bear was lumbering away, keening as though in pain. Gretel's chest tore she was breathing so quickly.

"Hansel," she panted. Her brother was sprawled on the forest floor. He was still. Too still. Then, with a groan, Hansel picked himself up.

"Gretel?"

"I'm fine. Are you hurt? There was blood— Oh!"

Hansel's jerkin had ripped across the shoulder. Crimson bloomed across the cloth. He circled his arm, then flexed his hand. "I don't know," he groaned. "It happened so quickly."

Gretel didn't like the greyness creeping across his face. She had no way of knowing if the wound was one of those minor ones that bled a lot or something worse, and no way of treating it, either. "The bear is gone."

Hansel started to tremble. "Gretel? Am I dying? Because I can smell that cake that Mother used to make, and there is mist everywhere."

Shock. He was going into shock. Gretel hadn't seen it before but she knew people could die if they were sufficiently shaken. A bead of sweat trickled into her eyes. "Hansel, we should leave," she said. "Hansel! Can you hear me?"

"Oh," he gasped. And there it was, only a few feet away. A little house. It appeared in a blink. With it came sudden silence, as though the birdsong had been abruptly shrouded.

Gretel glanced at Hansel. He did not run, even though he must have realized where they were. "We should leave," she said. She felt as though she were in a fog; even speaking was difficult. "Please, Hansel. Take my hand and we'll walk away."

"Am I dreaming?" Hansel said thickly. "It really is gingerbread?"

Gretel looked at the rich, orange-brown walls. Sloped roof, tiles dripping with white icing. Glowing, colourful window panels made from coloured sugar sheets rather than glass. Decorative patterns drawn in white icing that surrounded the window frames and doors. It really did look good enough to eat.

"No, Hansel," Gretel said. "Those drips you take as frosting are ice, and the windows are coloured glass rather than boiled sweets."

Hansel closed his eyes. "I'm so hungry." He gave a faint laugh. "I wish we could eat it." He stepped forward, pointing. "Look.

There's a basket of gingerbread by the door. I need to… It smells so good."

He sat heavily on the wall by the front door, wobbling a little. Gretel picked up the basket that sat enticingly on a tree stump and stared down into it. The gingerbread inside was still warm. Hansel reached inside, bloodied fingers closing round one of the biscuits. It had been cut into the shape of a person, with eyes and lips and hair iced by a shaky hand. Hansel squinted at it.

"Funny," he mumbled.

"What is?"

"It looks like Bertolf Fischer."

The last boy before Jakob who had disappeared.

"Don't be silly, Hansel," said Gretel sharply. "It doesn't look anything like Bertolf. It's a gingerbread man. You are in shock." She glanced around. "We must go. It's dangerous here. You should put it back—"

"You must be hungry too. Please eat, Gretel. If I don't make it, you'll need all your strength." Hansel tried to press the gingerbread man into Gretel's palm. She stepped away, shaking her head.

"No, Hansel – put it down. We'll find somewhere else to rest."

Hansel bit into the gingerbread man, chewed and swallowed. Then he wolfed the rest down, moaning as the spices and sweetness came alive in his mouth. Almost before he had swallowed, his eyelids drooped. Alarmed, Gretel threaded an arm around him.

"Hansel?"

"Sleepy." Her brother swayed against her. Unprepared for his full weight, Gretel staggered backwards and managed to lay him down on the grass. Hansel's head lolled back. She watched him, heart thumping.

"Hansel? Please, Hansel, we need to leave, can't you understand..."

This wasn't right, surely. She knelt down, placing her ear to his mouth. Warm breath tickled her cheek. She closed her eyes for a second. He was alive.

The front door swung open. The scent of ginger and spice and sugar filled the air. A bent figure shuffled out.

"Well, well, well," crowed Esther. "What have we here?"

NOW

GRETEL LEAVES WESTERLEEN

Two Days After the Return

Gretel had never been in a carriage before, but she tried not to let that show as she clambered up the steps. Inside, she settled on to the cushioned seat, and Lord Fabian and Jakob joined her. Outside, everyone in Westerleen had come to bid her farewell, lining the lanes. The carriage gave a little jolt – Gretel's bandaged hand flew out to steady herself – and then they were off.

Gretel started waving to people but swiftly felt ridiculous, so settled for smiling instead. By the time they broke free of Westerleen, her cheeks felt as though they were splitting. When she glanced back, the people she had known all her life had gathered by the edge of the village, watching.

I might never see any of them again. For a moment, she felt unsteady, like a child learning to walk. Then, joy flooded her.

She was getting out!

For the next ten minutes, the only sound was the clopping of hooves. Lord Fabian angled his body in such a way to make it clear that he did not wish to engage in conversation. Jakob watched the trees and bushes and undergrowth bounce by.

How astonishing it is to suddenly be free, she thought. She had walked up this track before, but rarely. Hansel had been further, but not by much. Gretel had not been sure what to make of their goodbye. Hansel had hugged her, but he would not meet her eyes.

Was he having doubts about what had happened in the cottage too? Surely not – Hansel was always the last person to notice when something didn't add up. More likely he felt funny about her stealing the limelight. He'd let everyone think him the hero the night they'd returned, hadn't he?

Her goodbye to her father had almost been worse. The expression on his face was one she had never seen before: fear.

When Gretel ventured a goodbye, he had said, "It's best that you leave. I can see you do not belong."

Ilse had not appeared. Her punishment was at present undecided. *I wonder if I will find out what befell her,* Gretel thought. Only a handful of villagers were literate, and Hansel was unaware Gretel could read so was unlikely to dictate a letter to her. The only way she would hear news was probably from merchants and traders. The two-hour carriage ride made Lord Fabian's manor too far to visit easily.

Not that they would want to, if they knew what she had done.

THEN

THE WITCH'S STORY

*The Morning After the Second Abandonment
and Two Weeks Before the Return*

Esther craned her neck to inspect Hansel, leaning heavily on her stick. She nudged his arm with her toe.

"Skinny," she commented.

Gretel's head was still spinning from the bear attack, and the cottage's sudden appearance. "Why is he sleeping? Was there something in that gingerbread?"

Esther sighed, rolling her eyes as though Gretel was stupid. "You should mind your manners, girl. How about a 'good morning, Esther'?"

"What have you done to him? Please tell me. And it's Gretel."

Esther made a tutting noise. "Well, *Gretel*, I suggest you use your brain. How do you imagine I managed to lure all those strapping young boys into my cottage, when they know I am a wicked witch who eats people? It's certainly not by asking nicely."

She threw back her head and laughed. In the stillness that surrounded them it seemed very loud indeed. Gretel stared at the plate, and the leftover crumbs. A trap.

"Hunger," she said. "You know they will be powerless to resist such food."

"I feed them as though they are dogs," said Esther. "Boys always think with their bellies. By then, it's too late. Don't look so scared. It is only a harmless sleeping draught."

Gretel knelt by Hansel, pushing his hair off his face. He felt hot. Was Esther lying about the sleeping draught? "What about the bear? Was that you, too?"

"You think I control the forest predators? *Tsk, tsk.* I am no animal charmer. Bears often lurk around here. They're attracted by the bones I throw them, sometimes innards that are of no use. I think of them as my pets."

Bones and innards of her victims? Tossed away without a second thought. Gretel thought she might heave yesterday's thin stew all over her shoes.

Esther nudged Hansel again, this time his shoulder. "Is that a wound? I don't like how it looks."

"I'll wash and bandage it."

"Do you think he deserves your pity? If he could reverse your positions, he would in a heartbeat. All men are selfish."

Hansel wasn't. He'd tried to offer the gingerbread to her – even though he was the one hurt. "I don't like seeing people in pain."

"Then you are weak."

The bitter smell of blood cut through the sugary air and made Gretel feel sicker still. To her relief, Hansel's wound did not appear to be as bad as she'd feared. The blood seeping through his jerkin was feeble. Once clean and bound, it should heal by itself. She was more concerned about what had been in the gingerbread.

"If I shove him straight in the oven, we won't need to treat the wound," said Esther. "It might not be worth fattening him up if that's going to fester. Better cook a skinny lad than hack an infested arm off a fatter one. It would be a kindness."

Gretel recoiled. So the stories were true; the witch wanted to cook Hansel. Esther was mad, quite mad – and every bit as dangerous as the rumours said.

She couldn't let it happen. Buy time – that was what she must do, until Hansel was better and could defend himself, and Gretel could figure out what best to do. "It wouldn't be kind, though," she said, talking fast. "Not really. You said yourself, he's skinny, he's… I am confident the wound will heal. Really."

Aware she was babbling, Gretel closed her mouth. She waited for the witch to laugh again or tell her she was wrong. Instead, Esther grunted, and turned to hobble back inside.

"Bring him inside, girl."

Gretel felt her brother's forehead again; still burning up. Perhaps Esther was right. If there was no way out of this, it would be better for Hansel to never wake up; never know his fate.

"Girl!" Esther shouted. "I said, drag him in."

Gretel glanced back at the way they had come, then at her motionless brother. Moments passed. She clutched Hansel's limp wrists as best she could with her stiff fingers and used the weight of her body to heave him inside. Hansel moaned as his body bumped over the raised doorstep and Gretel bit back a "sorry".

Warmth enveloped Gretel and, despite everything, for a second she thought she might cry in relief. She laid Hansel down on the rug, then, as soon as she could flex her fingers properly again, slipped out to draw fresh water from the stream which ran through the garden. Esther was in the rocking chair when she returned. She watched Gretel smack down the bucket, crouch down by her brother and dab away the blood.

"If the wound isn't showing signs of healing by tomorrow, I'll fire up the oven," she said. "I prefer not keeping them locked up for too long, and I can't see your brother putting on flesh quickly."

I prefer not keeping them locked up for too long. Gretel closed her eyes. That answered the question of what had happened to the lord's son, then. What could she say? *Be agreeable. That was safest.* Stumbling over the words, she said, "You'd be surprised. Hansel eats like a horse when he can. Soon he'll be nice and round, I promise you."

Hansel's wound looked better now. Esther shrugged when Gretel asked for bandages so she tore a strip off a cleaning cloth and wrapped it tight.

"Now," Esther said. "You must move him."

Gretel eyed Hansel uneasily. He was grey and limp – he needed to be somewhere comfortable to recover. "Where should I put him?"

"There," Esther sounded impatient as she waved her hand towards the door. "Quickly, he's coming round."

Through the side door was a narrow corridor. It smelled fusty and dank. At one end was a staircase.

"Where now?" Gretel called. "Down the stairs? Or…"

"Open the door to your left," Esther commanded. Gretel did so. This room was tiny, no more than a cupboard, with the narrowest of narrow windows. Inside was a blanket and a bucket. Gretel blanched.

"This is where you mean to keep him?"

"You expect me to provide a bed?"

"I'm sorry, Hansel," Gretel whispered. She hefted Hansel inside, laying him down on the blanket. It was threadbare and no doubt filthy, and would provide precious little comfort.

Perhaps the oven would have been better after all.

Gretel hesitated. She could leave Hansel, escape the cottage and run, far from Esther and Westerleen. The witch might be planning to cook her too. The floorboards from the corridor creaked. Gretel jumped. A thought leapt into her head: *the witch means to close the door on me!* She dived into the hallway, almost smacking into the opposite wall. Esther, standing some paces away, raised her eyebrows.

"Careful, Gretel. I'd hate for you to hurt yourself."

Gretel rubbed the side of her face, not sure if Esther was mocking her or issuing some kind of veiled threat. Esther closed the door to Hansel's cell and slid a key into the lock. The click as it turned sounded very final.

"There," Esther said in a bright voice. "That went well, didn't it?"

"Without a hitch," whispered Gretel.

Esther looped the key, which was attached to a cord, around her neck. She snaked her hand on to Gretel's shoulder. Gretel just about managed not to flinch.

"You are doing the right thing." To Gretel's surprise, the witch's voice was soft. "I was like you once. Clever and angry. Unless you fight, you will be trampled underfoot. One boy's life for a better future is not a trade you should trouble your conscience with. There are hundreds of other useless boys just like your brother. He will be no loss." She paused. "You did tell me you didn't like him."

Gretel thought of Hansel and the small kindnesses he had showed her – like appreciating the unpleasant, watery soup she'd made the other day. Best not to think of that.

"I don't like him," she said. "And I don't regret what I've done."

"Good." The weight of Esther's hand lifted. Gretel eyed the witch, taking in the wide, toothless mouth, the wizened skin and the beady eyes. It was hard to imagine her as anything other than old. "How were you like me?"

"I wanted more. I was not content to do as I was expected to. People didn't like that. They started to laugh whenever they saw me, and mock my ways. Soon I was a total outcast. Not because I had done anything wrong, but because I made others uneasy."

Gretel knew all about being an outcast – but she had never thought that the boys who called her names did so because they saw her as some kind of threat. The thought unsettled her. "How did you end up here?"

For a second, she was afraid she had spoken out of turn. This was the wicked witch, after all. In this moment, though, Esther did not look fearsome – more like a weary woman who had seen a lot. She gestured Gretel to the kitchen. They settled down opposite each other, Esther in the rocking chair, Gretel on a stool.

"I tolerated the way people treated me too long," the witch said. "I tried to be a good Westerleen girl because, like you, I did not think I had a choice. Precious good that did me." Her eyes went misty. "A cruel husband. A father who did not care. Brothers who mocked me. Friends and sisters who shrugged and told me to make the best of things, and that I worsened my lot by being difficult. Many wasted years I tried to follow that advice. One day I had enough. I walked into the trees and fully embraced being an outcast."

The stories Gretel had heard claimed that Esther had poisoned her husband, set alight the cottage where her father and brothers were sleeping, then vanished into the forest. If true, she had done a terrible thing. Many terrible things. And yet … surely some of the responsibility lay with those who had made her life unbearable?

Gretel fiddled with the end of her braid. She felt dangerous admitting it, even to herself, but there was much she related to in Esther's story. Maybe in a few years that could have been her. Who knew?

"I cannot quite imagine embracing being an outcast," she admitted. "And yet…"

"… here you are," Esther said, and Gretel shifted. She was both drawn to Esther and discomfited at the same time. The only other person who had ever finished her sentences had been Hansel, when they were small and so close you never saw one without the other.

"Being a witch does not require any special skills, you know," said Esther. "Only a brain. I have a library of books in this cottage.

They will open your mind and take you to places you have never dreamed of. You'd like to see those, wouldn't you?"

"How do you know I can even read?"

"Witch's powers," she said with a wink.

Gretel wondered if young Esther, too, had found a way of secretly teaching herself letters.

Esther reclined further into her chair. "Stay here with me and I shall reveal all soon enough. You've brought me what I asked for, and that bodes well for the future. There is a whole world I can open the doors to, Gretel, like nothing you have ever known." She paused, and something shifted in the atmosphere. "If it pleases me, that is."

And there it was. A subtle threat; a reminder that, despite their similarities, Esther was still a witch, and a powerful one at that – one who must not be displeased.

NOW

ARRIVAL AT THE MANOR HOUSE

Two Days After the Return

By the time the small town where Lord Fabian's manor nestled came into view, snow was wisping downwards. Gretel, who had been fighting nausea brought on by the backwards and forwards motion of the carriage, sat up straighter. This place did not look that different to Westerleen, though houses and cottages stood closer together and a variety of shops lined the main street instead of market stalls. Still, it was livelier than she was used to.

They approached tall gates that gleamed even in the dull winter's light. The carriage passed through them and came to a stop by a fountain. Gretel allowed Jakob to help her alight, aware that from now onwards they would be watched.

She gazed upwards at the manor. It looked to be three storeys high, with round windows that protruded from the roof and a balcony supported by sturdy pillars. Neatly trimmed ivy climbed up the walls. At the top, just below the roof, was a strip of stone etched with carvings that told some kind of story, and in front of every window were wooden boxes that in warmer times Gretel guessed would contain flowers.

Almost like a palace from a story. Gretel wished her mother could see her now.

Jakob leaned close to Gretel's ear as his father strode ahead. "Say little, smile and ignore anyone who stares," he murmured.

"Just like in Westerleen, then," Gretel said. "It's a good job I am well-practised."

Jakob laughed softly. The great doors opened as they approached, and warmth swallowed them. Gretel found herself standing in an entrance hall with what felt like an impossibly high ceiling and walls hung with colourful tapestries. It was illuminated by many candles, though in summer she imagined the window at the top of the staircase would throw down plenty of light. Doors led off everywhere. How many rooms must this house have? Gretel's head started to spin. Never had she felt plainer or more out of place.

A stately-looking woman with hair piled high on her head breezed out of the closest door. She curtseyed to Lord Fabian, then enveloped Jakob in her arms.

"Now I can breathe properly," she cried. "I have been beside myself ever since your father sent word you had vanished. Did no one tell you not to go into that forest? Or did you not listen? Why are you always, *always* so difficult?"

Jakob's mother burst into tears. Lord Fabian sighed, shepherding his wife and son to one of the open doors. Gretel found herself alone in the hallway, in the way of servants bringing in luggage. She had no idea where she was supposed to go.

"May I help?" she asked a female servant bustling past with their cloaks. "You look busy, I could…"

The girl blinked at her, like a startled animal, then she scurried off. Gretel stepped out of the way, her back bumping the side of the stairs, and her face burning.

The door Jakob and his parents had vanished behind opened. The girl who appeared was older than Gretel, and so like Jakob to look at that she could only be his sister.

She gave Gretel a nervous smile. "You are the one we have to thank for my brother's safe return, then. My father sent word. Hello, Gretel. I am Ottillie."

Gretel curtseyed. She was not sure how to speak to Jakob's sister, but Ottillie seemed friendlier than anyone else so she decided to be direct. "Where should I be? No one has shown me where to go."

"Then allow me. I have arranged a room for you and a few dresses that should do for now. Come."

Upstairs, Gretel found herself in a bedroom with a creaking floor and a bed twice the size of her mattress at home. The room was not especially grand, but wall tapestries kept in the warmth and the window overlooked the forecourt. This was the second time in almost as few weeks that she had been welcomed into a new home – if welcomed was the right word for how Esther had received her.

Ottillie closed the door. Her brown eyes were level and serious.

"I am not quite sure what is going on," she said. "But Jakob is my favourite brother and I am grateful he is safe. So, as far as I am concerned, you are welcome. I will do my best to help you in any way I can."

"Thank you. You are very kind."

A silence developed. Ottillie fidgeted with her hair. Then she said, "May I be honest? A promise seems a funny kind of reward for saving Jakob's life. What am I missing?"

"I didn't manipulate him if that's what you mean," said Gretel, then, catching Ottille's cheeks colour, she added quickly, "I don't mean to be blunt or rude. I... I am not used to speaking to..."

"Someone like me?" The ghost of a smile drifted on to Ottillie's mouth. "I am not used to speaking to someone like you, so in that respect we are even. And I did not mean to insult you. I do not think it would be possible to force Jakob into doing something he objected to, however hard our father may try. He is headstrong, not to mention difficult."

If Gretel had a gold coin for every time someone had described *her* as headstrong or difficult, she would have a treasure trove by now. "I think Jakob wants to show your father he cannot be controlled."

"You are happy with this arrangement? Being here?" Gretel hesitated, and Ottillie came closer. "I know what it is like to be somewhere you do not belong and cannot escape."

The door swung open. Jakob appeared, scowling.

"I did not enjoy that," he said. "Mother is unhappy. She had all but arranged a match for me with some far-off lord's daughter, and she is beside herself that it won't happen. You had best avoid

185

her entirely, Gretel. She hates this even more than Father. He was issuing me with dozens of rules about how I am to behave around you." He made a huffing noise. "You would think, given I am his fifth son, that he would be more relaxed about what I do, but apparently not. Anyway."

Jakob went over to Ottillie and gave her a big hug.

"I missed you," he murmured. "I want to hear everything you have been doing while I was gone. May I have a moment to speak to Gretel first?"

Ottillie squeezed his shoulder as she stepped back.

"I have been so worried about her," Jakob said the moment door closed.

Gretel nodded. Jakob had told her all about Ottillie while in Esther's cottage. Ottillie had been dispatched to marry a nobleman her parents had brokered an advantageous deal with, but an outbreak of pox before the wedding and the subsequent death of her betrothed had put pay to those plans. The man Ottillie was supposed to marry had a terrible reputation and Jakob had tried his best to get his father to reconsider.

"Perhaps the next arrangement your parents make will be kinder to her," Gretel said.

Jakob scowled. "It had better be. Honestly, the way Ottillie was expected to simply succumb to what would have been a miserable life… I hated it. I know you were in the same position. Worse, even."

All that awaits you is misery. Gretel looked away.

"Listen to me, spouting all this radical talk." Jakob paused to draw breath. "Unless all four of my brothers and my five nephews all have the misfortune to perish before their time and I miraculously inherit Father's lordship, I will never have the power to change anything. At least I can help you change your life, though."

He smiled, somewhat awkwardly. Without warning, Gretel's face went hot with shame. Would he feel the same if he knew the truth about the decisions she had made?

The door creaked open. It was Ottillie.

"Jakob, Mother wants you," she said. "I don't think she wants you and Gretel left alone together."

Jakob rolled his eyes. He swept an extravagant bow, then left.

Ottillie tilted her head. "His near brush with death seems to have done him good," she mused. "He seems less restless than usual. Whatever scheme you two have afoot, it's clearly a better use of his time than his previous hobbies."

"What previous hobbies?" said Gretel immediately.

Ottillie looked a little startled. "Nothing sinister, just a lot of causing trouble for the sake of it. Father found it tiresome."

Tiresome. Lord Fabian had used that word when he had spoken to Jakob alone in The Green Gate: *I assume this is another childish attempt at rebellion, one of your tiresome little games. What will the peasant girl do when you grow bored of this?*

Was she just another one of Jakob's games? A way to annoy his father? Well, if so, at least he was helping her. Perhaps he was going to be a friend to her after all. Then, Gretel remembered the decision she had made, the first time she had visited Esther's cottage.

THEN

ESTHER'S GUESTS

*The Morning After the Second Abandonment
and Two Weeks Before the Return*

Esther began to hum under her breath, rocking to and fro on her chair. The conversation about her past, it seemed, was over. Gretel could not read her mood, so waited instead. At least here in the kitchen it was warm and comfortable. Her toes were only just thawing.

Eventually, Esther flexed her fingers and Gretel winced at the cracking noise. "How is your cooking, Gretel?"

"How do you think?" said Gretel. "I told you, cooking and cleaning is all I ever do."

"Help yourself to whatever you like from my pantry and conjure something up for our guests. The richer the better. We need meat on their bones. A hearty meal, followed by some of Esther's sweet treats."

Guests. Gretel's stomach turned. What a twisted word to refer to her captives by. Mechanically, she rose and sought an apron. Perhaps years of nothing but her own company and that of terrified boys had turned the witch's mind. Gretel wondered how long it had taken Esther to become numb to the horror of luring lost, hungry children into her oven. If she had ever had a conscience, it must have been stripped away, like the muscle and fat from her victim's bones.

And to think, for a few minutes Gretel had forgotten who she was speaking to! It still seemed unreal that coming here had been her choice.

Gretel rolled up her sleeves and selected a variety of ingredients from the pantry – a cool store cupboard crammed full of loaded shelves and stacked baskets. Being confronted with so much food made her knees shake. Slabs of butter, a pitcher of thick cream, grains, flour, fine dried fruits, wine, vegetables, preserved fish, some kind of meat sausage, even pears, which Gretel had not seen for years. There was enough to feed an entire village here!

It was as much as Gretel could manage not to seize a handful of dried fruit and stuff it into her mouth. Her stomach was hollow, and the sight of such wonderful ingredients made her light-headed. She was too afraid to ask if she could eat herself before cooking. This felt like a test.

Conscious that Esther was watching, Gretel got to work making savoury pastry and stewing sausage, potato and vegetables to fill a pie. Heavy, hearty fare, exactly as requested – and exactly the kind of thing Gretel had been dreaming of for weeks. By the time the pie was in the oven, she felt weak from kneading and chopping. Esther shuffled over to inspect what she had made, sniffing.

"Not bad," she said. "Throw another log on that fire. Are you hungry? Or is that something I need to ask? As soon as it is ready you may eat. Once you're sated, take your brother his."

Logs were piled next to the fire. Gretel tossed a couple on to the flames. For the first time she realized she was trembling. Why? Because it was torture to handle food when her belly was empty? Because Hansel was injured, imprisoned and vulnerable, and she could not help him? Because already the witch was not what she expected? For all of those reasons, perhaps.

The moment the pastry crisped, Gretel served herself pie and ate in silence. She could not finish her portion – months of eating little must have shrunk her stomach – but by the time she laid down her knife, she felt stronger and less like she might collapse.

If I stay here, I won't want for food ever again, Gretel thought.

Esther shook her head when she saw the slice of pie Gretel had cut for Hansel.

"More than that, girl. He'll never get fat on half-portions. Slap a wedge of cake on there too."

"Why is it so important that he gets fat?"

"So I can eat him, of course – don't you know the stories?"

"You barely have any teeth."

"You have no sense of humour, girl." But Esther laughed despite that. Gretel narrowed her eyes. The witch had a full pantry, including meat – she did not need to steal the boys for food. Something else was afoot.

Gretel took the prepared plate to Hansel's cell. He was lying where she had dragged him, but he was murmuring and twitching, clearing coming round. With relief, Gretel noted that the wound didn't seem to have bled far through her makeshift bandage. His forehead felt cooler, too.

Saved from a bear bite, only to perish in that oven. It was too difficult to look at her brother so she quickly positioned the plate on the floor and retreated.

"Make a second plate," said Esther as Gretel joined her in the kitchen.

Gretel froze.

"A second plate?" Her voice came out sounding distorted and high-pitched. "For you?"

"No! I have another guest, in the cellar."

Another guest. Esther had said she preferred not to keep the boys captive too long. Gretel had assumed that meant…

I was wrong.

"As you wish," she said, in a small voice. "Where is the cellar?"

It was good to ask that, Gretel thought numbly. Esther could never suspect she already knew.

"The staircase is at the end of the corridor where your brother is."

Gretel's hand shook as she cut a generous wedge of pie. It took three attempts to light the candle. Wiping sweat from her forehead, Gretel entered the corridor, passing Hansel's door. The staircase that led to the cellar was rickety and uneven, creaking as Gretel descended, balancing the plate in one hand and candle in the other. It was wet down here, and smelled even worse than it had above. Gretel sneezed. No one deserved to be kept in such conditions.

Just beyond the bottom step was a door, with a barred recess cut into it. Gretel gathered courage. Then she called, "Hello?"

Thump. Hands curled round the bars. Her candle picked out a face. The wild eyes staring back at her were Jakob's, face streaked with dirt. Gretel closed her eyes a second. So he *was* alive.

"You!" Jakob breathed. "I have never been more pleased to see anyone in my life before. Let me out. Please. I shouldn't be here."

Why hadn't Esther killed him yet? Wordlessly, Gretel unlocked the door, pushing it open just wide enough to lay down the plate. Jakob's foot shot forwards to wedge it open but Gretel was quicker. The clang as the door closed was very loud in the silence.

"You're working for her?" Jakob's face bobbed back at the bars. Gretel skirted a look up the staircase, afraid Esther might be listening, but she could hear and see nothing apart from silent darkness.

"No, I'm not working for her," she said in a low voice. "I'm…"

What was she?

"… here," she finished.

"Not a captive?"

"She only takes boys. My brother is in another cell. She wants me to cook and clean, I think. How did you end up here? I told you she was dangerous. Why didn't you listen?"

"Believe me, I wish I had. Can you get me out? You know how rich my father is. He will be very grateful."

Gretel backed away, shaking her head.

"Please." His tone was urgent now. "I know you are afraid of her but she's just an old woman and can barely see. We can rescue your brother and get away from here."

"I can't talk now," she whispered, and ran.

Something woke Gretel. For a moment she panicked, confused as to why she lay in a bed that wasn't hers. Then, it all came back: the drugged gingerbread, and the cottage, and the boy in the cellar she had presumed dead.

Outside, from the forest, came snarling. Some beast fighting another. Perhaps it wasn't a bad thing it had woken her. She hesitated, then silently she slipped her feet into her boots and drew her cloak around her shoulders. The room Esther had given her to sleep in was small and plainly furnished, but comfortable and warm, with a soft, feather mattress – and no Hansel to disturb her. The witch had even tossed several gowns on to the bed before retiring to her own chambers, saying Gretel was welcome to them.

Gretel gathered the cloak around her shoulders now, inching open the door and listening. From nearby came loud, wheezing snores.

She won't be waking up anytime soon, Gretel thought, having earlier witnessed Esther swallow a sleeping draught. Still, she was cautious as she crept downstairs and lit a candle. First, she sought Hansel's cell, but stopped when she heard heavy breathing. What was she thinking? There was nothing Gretel could say that would help Hansel any more. The deed was done – over. He might as well be in the oven already. Nothing good would happen if they did speak, except to make her feel even worse than she already did. *Probably best I let him sleep.*

The cellar was just as freezing by night as it had been by day, and even more intimidating. As Gretel approached the bottom step there was scrabbling from within.

Gretel made a shushing sound. "You'll wake her."

Jakob's face appeared at the bars. "Are you here to let me out?"

"I don't have the key. She keeps it on her person."

"Why didn't you free me earlier?"

"Esther knew I was down here. Letting you out without a plan isn't going to help anyone." Gretel raised the candle so she could see him properly. "Why are you still here?"

"You mean, why hasn't she eaten me?" Jakob laughed humourlessly. "I don't know. But all she ever does is feed me, so I assume that rumour is true enough."

"I'm not sure if it is that simple. She has plenty to eat."

"I toss much of what she gives me to the rats. She is completely mad. Didn't even react when I told her who my father was!"

"I don't think Esther cares about such things. She seems to live by her own rules."

Jakob's eyebrows drew together sharply. "You almost sound as though you approve."

Gretel shot him a glare. "Of a witch who kills children? Don't say such ridiculous things." Jakob was not wrong though. Wasn't living by her own rules what Gretel wanted, too? Esther was proof it was possible. Women could take control of their own lives.

"How did you come to be captured?"

Jakob rubbed his hand over his face. "I didn't want to come on the progress with my father. He said it was about time I learned more about the villages he governs, but really he wanted to get me away from home."

"Why?"

Jakob hesitated. Gretel sensed if she had asked under different circumstances he would have refused to answer. But she could also

197

tell that he wanted to talk. "He and my mother were marrying my sister to someone abhorrent, and I was trying to stop them."

He launched into Ottillie's story. Gretel listened, rocking backwards and forwards on her heels.

"But before the wedding could take place, he died of the pox," said Jakob. "Ottillie is back at home now. Father wants me out of the way while Mother seeks new matches." A pause. Then vulnerability crept into his voice. "They want to do the same for me."

"Arrange a marriage? Isn't that something you expect, though?"

"Not this soon. They didn't make matches for my brothers until they were older than I am. They're trapped now, doing exactly what my father commands. No freedom. I always imagined I'd somehow be able to avoid all that."

Gretel thought of Cristoph, and what marrying him would have meant for her. How odd that the rich boy had the same fears as she did.

Jakob continued. "Visiting all these villages is supposed to tame me, I think, presumably through loneliness and boredom. If Father really involved me, it might be different, but I am expected to listen in silence. And, well, Ottillie says I am incapable of keeping my mouth shut. I was so angry by the time we reached your village,

I wanted to teach my father a lesson." He rubbed his jaw. "Hiding in the forest for a few hours so he would be scared the witch had me seemed a good idea. Then I got lost, and by the time the cottage appeared, I was so tired and cold. There was gingerbread outside. Somehow, I couldn't resist it."

"The same happened to Hansel."

"How did you end up here?"

Now Gretel hesitated. What exactly to say? *Facts,* she thought. *I will tell Jakob only things that cannot be disproved.* "Our father abandoned us in the forest."

"Oh. I didn't think that kind of thing happened any more. Sorry." Jakob sounded awkward. Gretel waved the apology away.

"Hansel was drugged and put in the cell. I think the witch means to keep me as a servant," she said.

"You have free rein of the house, then," said Jakob.

"For now. She does not trust me fully. If she knew we were having this conversation, I would be locked up too."

"Let us not be discovered then. You are my best hope of getting out of this alive." Abruptly, he said, "For what it's worth, I'm sorry I was so rude when we spoke before. I was in a bad mood and said things I shouldn't have."

That conversation felt a lifetime ago, and so unimportant.

"What is your life like when you're not on a progress?" Gretel asked curiously.

Jakob revealed that until recently he'd been living in one of Lord Fabian's other houses in far-off Levalliers City. He described it all – from the grand houses and turrets, to the theatres and shops, and the narrow, cramped lanes where he was not supposed to go.

"I sneak off there anyway," he said, smiling for the first time. "If my father listened to anything I say, I'd tell him to do the same. He would learn a lot about ordinary people."

For a moment there, Gretel had felt as though she too were in the city, with Jakob's words bringing the pictures in her mother's book to life. "Have you been to the university?"

"Yes, several times. At some point soon I will probably go there myself. They accept students our age."

"Is it true that they admit women?"

He inclined his head. "You ask as though the world depends on it."

Gretel glanced away. "Do not belittle me."

"I wasn't." Jakob leaned forwards, so close that his nose practically touched the bars. His eyes were almost as dark as his hair. "I'm starting to understand you better, that is all. Our dreams say a lot about us."

Gretel suddenly wondered what Esther would say about her university dream. Laugh scornfully, probably. She tilted her chin upwards, squaring her shoulders. "I can read. I have a keen mind, when I am allowed to exercise it. Why shouldn't I want an education?"

"Well said." He flashed a smile. "I like people who challenge the rules."

"You don't think it foolish for a peasant girl to aspire to more?"

"Gretel, I could not care less about any of that. If I ever gain any kind of power, I fully intend to tear things up. Capable people are stuck in miserable lives because of old-fashioned traditions. I've been taught by many tutors, some from far-off places, and they have opened my mind. Everyone should have that opportunity. Boys and girls." He paused. "Did you know that further east girls are educated along with boys? Those women take on many of the jobs men do and society seems to function just fine. We could learn from them. I wonder sometimes if my father is afraid, and that is why he prefers to keep everything the same. There is so much I would like to change." The smile that had crept on to his face faded. "If I ever get out of here, that is."

Gretel became aware of the drip of water, and the coldness radiating through her feet. She had almost forgotten where they were. Inside, she felt fierce. Despite herself, she found she was warming to Jakob. How could she not, after hearing a speech like that?

And he would die here if she did not help him. "Listen, if I can, I will get you back to Westerleen safely, but you have to trust me." The words came out in a rush, and Gretel was unable to stop herself. "We don't know what Esther is capable of. I need a greater sense of that before doing anything."

Jakob's lips pressed into a thin line. "What if she drugs me?"

"When I deliver food, I will tell you which things were cooked by me, and you'll know they are safe to eat."

Jakob nodded slowly.

"My father is rich, as you know. If you really do get me out of here..." Jakob paused. "You'll have his gratitude. He is a good person to have on your side." Another pause. "If, in the process of freeing me, Esther met her doom somehow... After all, she is a monster. And when monsters are slain, my father rewards generously."

Gretel shot him a sharp look. "Are you telling me I should kill her?"

"All I am telling you is that bounty hunters make a fine profit by ridding the land of threats. The benefits could be great. It would not be difficult."

Their eyes met. Gretel understood exactly what Jakob was doing. *He doesn't trust me to save him and thinks a reward may act as persuasion.*

She wished he hadn't put the thought into her head. "I cannot kill someone, Jakob, but I will do my best to free you." She hesitated. "It was nice talking."

And – strangely – it had been. Jakob grunted, moving back to the blanket at the back of the cell.

"Goodnight then." He paused. "Please can you come again? I am going mad with nothing to do and no one but the rats to talk to."

"When I can." She wanted to offer him the candle but Esther might spot it. "Goodnight."

Back upstairs, in her room, Gretel closed the door and leaned against it. She placed a palm to her forehead. Hot.

Why did I go down there? she thought. Making such a dangerous promise, too! Gretel was shocked at herself for acting so rashly … and out of compassion. All Gretel's life people had called her cold. Now she was responsible for Jakob.

Coming here was supposed to have been a means to an end. An escape, at any cost. Simple.

And now it was anything but.

NOW

GRETEL'S NEW LIFE

Two Weeks After the Return

The first, then second week of Gretel's stay in the manor house passed quietly. Gretel began to feel out the boundaries of her new life. To her relief, she was not simply left to pass the time in her room and was instead permitted to join some of Ottillie's lessons with her tutor. These were not as interesting as Gretel had hoped, mainly covering etiquette, needlework and writing. It was a pleasant surprise to discover that her grasp of reading was equal to Ottillie's though, and, in some instances, her knowledge superior, for she had a better memory and was quicker to grasp new concepts.

Jakob also arranged to smuggle her into the language lessons taught to the sons of his eldest brother. Learning a foreign tongue was entirely new to Gretel, but it did not take long for her to understand the fundamentals.

"So, you are not too proud to share a desk with children?" Jakob asked her one evening. They sat either side of a chess board, with Ottillie writing letters over the other side of the room. Jakob was keen to teach her the game. Gretel pretended to be a complete novice. It was better he did not know that she had played chess with Esther.

She smiled. "I am not proud at all, as you well know."

"Hopefully Father won't find out and stop you. Luckily for us, he's been far too busy to pay you any attention – or me, for that matter. My nephews and their tutor won't betray us. I've made sure they'll keep silent."

"How?"

"I shan't tell." He winked. "I have to have some secrets. Nothing sinister, though."

"I thought you were incapable of keeping your mouth shut," she said, and at that he laughed. Gretel liked the sound of his laugh, and she was hearing it quite a lot. She and Jakob spent most of their leisure time together. He had shown her around the manor and the surrounding town, explaining its history, entertaining her with stories from his childhood and waiting patiently while she marvelled at shops and market stalls. On finer days, they took long walks, including to the closest river. Gretel was touched Jakob had remembered how much she liked water. They were always accompanied by servants, but Gretel was usually so absorbed in conversation that she forgot they were being watched.

She picked up one of the chess pieces. "Can I move this here?"

"No, because it is a knight," said Jakob

Gretel slid another piece forwards. Jakob immediately hopped his rook over her queen.

"Bad move, Gretel."

"I'm learning."

"I tire of these lessons," Esther had snapped. "Chess is a game played by men with more money than sense anyway."

Then how did you come to know it? *Gretel had wondered, but she did not ask. There was so much about Esther's long, fascinating life she would probably never uncover.*

"That suits me. I prefer our other lessons," she'd said, and that had made Esther smile.

"Quite right," she had crooned. *"They are far more ... unique."*

Unsettled by the memory, Gretel stood.

"Excuse me," she said. "I forgot; I have a letter to write."

"Can't it wait until the game is finished?" asked Jakob. "Or are you tired of losing?"

"I would rather do it now. Sorry."

Jakob sighed but did not appear too annoyed. He picked up a book instead. Gretel went to the writing desk Ottillie had just vacated. Her palm hovered over the quill. Should she send a letter to Hansel? It had been on her mind since her arrival. Her brother only recognized a few basic words but there were other villagers who could read it to him – and pen a reply. Perhaps Hansel could let her know news of Ilse. Gretel was less worried about Cristoph – he cared about his reputation, so would probably make a grand show of forgetting her. If he stopped to think, he might even be secretly relieved she was gone. But Ilse had sworn revenge. She had meant it. And Ilse was both ruthless and determined...

Even if Hansel did not give her the reassurance she sought, it would still be good to hear from him. Gretel thought of her brother often.

Her mind went back to that fateful afternoon a few days after she'd watched Brida and her friends tell fortunes, the day before she and Hansel had gone into the forest together. She had emerged from the forest after having been absent the entire day – without the bundle that Cristoph had spotted her carrying earlier. She had been praying to return home without being spotted, but she had been unlucky...

Laughter met Gretel's ears as she broke from the trees at the edge of Westerleen. Hansel and his friends were tossing stones at an old archery target. Hansel was the last person she wanted to see. What bad luck. There was no way Gretel could avoid them, and she was wary of hiding and waiting for them to move on. So, hoping she remained invisible as usual, she passed by, trying to act like she had every reason to be strolling about when normally she would be elbow-deep in chores.

And, of course, Hansel spotted her. "Hey, Gretel!" he called. "What happened to you?"

Gretel was about to ask what he meant before realizing the boys were sniggering. Of course! Her gown was plastered with grime. A cobweb dangled from her hair. No doubt her face was filthy too.

"She looks like she's rolled around in mud like my father's pigs," said Rudolf Neydecker. "I thought your job was to clean, Gretel? Does that not include yourself?"

Hansel shook his head as more laughter erupted. He took Gretel's arm, tugging her away.

"Did something happen?" he asked in an undertone.

"I fell over in the shed," Gretel tried to keep her composure. "You would be surprised how much dirt there is in there."

"But you came from the forest."

Why of all days had Hansel chosen today to pay her attention? Most of the time he barely noticed what was under his nose.

"Because I needed fresh air, and saw little point in changing my gown," she snapped. "And before you ask, I don't care if people see me like this."

Hansel did not look entirely convinced. Her lie was a poor one. He said, "Maybe you should care. It is not the best idea to make yourself into even more of a joke."

"People laugh at me?"

"No," said Hansel, so quickly that he might as well have said "yes". "They just think you are difficult, and never seem happy."

All that awaits you is misery.

"Leave me alone, Hansel. Run back to your beloved friends."

Hansel's expression softened. "You miss her a lot, don't you?"

Gretel's fear and annoyance died as swiftly as fire doused by water. Her lip quivered. When was the last time anyone had mentioned Mother? Most of the time, it felt like she was forgotten.

Before she could stop herself, she said, "Don't you?"

"Of course," said Hansel simply. "We were all happier then. She was good at making everything seem better. Do you remember the story she made up about the king and the geese and the spinning wheel? How she would tell us a little each night and make us wait, however much we begged her for more?"

"She probably needed the day to plot what would happen next."

"I never thought of it like that."

Gretel kicked at a cluster of fallen leaves. Even her boots needed scrubbing. She was suddenly conscious of her brother beside her, who had no idea what was coming next. Mother had loved both her children, different though they were. For the first time ever, Gretel was glad Mother wasn't here. She was betraying her.

"Do you ever wonder what Mother would think if she could see us now?" she blurted out. "I think she'd be disappointed. All that talk of how we could do anything we wanted. How if we worked hard, we would get what we deserved. Instead, we're here, with no food, nothing to look forward to, only just scraping by."

Hansel drew an arm around her waist and squeezed. Gretel

went rigid. "Gretel, don't be angry, but don't you think that was just another of her stories?"

"She wanted more for us. She said so."

"She was encouraging us. That's what mothers do when children are small. Maybe you shouldn't have taken it to heart. I hear children saying those things all the time. The Weber girls think twin princes will trot into the village on white horses and marry them. Wilhelm Haufmann tells me he's going to run away and become a sailor, even though we live nowhere near the sea." Hansel paused. "I had dreams too – and they were every bit as silly – but I know that now, and it's all right. It is what happens, Gretel, when you stop being a child."

He sounded sickeningly reasonable. Gretel hated him for it.

All that awaits you is misery.

"We'll see about that," she said smartly.

"You'd find life easier if you saw sense," Hansel said. He bent down and retrieved a spinning top from the brambles. It had probably been cheerful once but its paint was faded now. "That's Sander Neydecker's toy. He'll be pleased it's not lost."

Gretel shook her head. "How do you know it belongs to Sander Neydecker? Lots of children have spinning tops."

"I recognize it. Children often tag along with us. I show them *how to whittle wood and identify bird calls. Sometimes I think I like their company best."*

"You should be a nurse." Gretel meant to rile him, but Hansel only shrugged.

"I don't think I have that choice."

Funny, thought Gretel now, running her hand along the writing desk, feeling its smooth grain. She hadn't paid Hansel's comment much heed, but today, with the clarity of distance and time, it came back to her. Perhaps it had never been Hansel himself she had objected to. It was what he had – what he could do – and the opportunities he had no interest in. His freedom.

And what Hansel most wanted to do was close to home. He'd always been happiest giving piggybacks and joining in imaginary games and comforting tearful children. Yet childcare was regarded as women's work. That was what *I don't think I have that choice* had meant. His freedom was an illusion.

The thought unsettled Gretel. *Perhaps we were not so different after all. He is the only person who truly knows how it felt to be left in that forest. And he remembers Mother.*

Mother, who wouldn't want there to be a divide between them and would have hated what Gretel had done, desperate or not.

Gretel picked up the quill. The words were not easy to find, but by the time the candle burned low, Gretel had filled two sides with her shaky but careful handwriting. She sought Ottillie.

"I have a letter to send to my brother," she said.

"Give it to me and I will pass it to one of the servants," Ottillie said. "So, you tired of indulging Jakob's passion for chess?"

"I am not the most obliging student. And he's not the most patient teacher."

"You looked to be enjoying yourself when I glanced over. Both of you, all smiles." Ottillie shot Gretel a demure, innocent kind of look. "He rarely gets along with people so well."

Was Ottillie implying what Gretel thought she was? Best ignored, Gretel decided. She held out the letter.

"Here. And thank you."

THEN

APPRENTICE TO THE WITCH

Six Days After the Second Abandonment
and Eight Days Before the Return

"I suppose you want to know what I do with those boys," said
Esther.

Gretel glanced over from where she stood, slicing pears. Six days
since she had arrived, and the kitchen was gleaming – years of grime
scrubbed away. The other rooms, too, were dust-free, from ceiling to
floor. The deep clean had included Esther's library. The witch had

not been exaggerating – the room, though not large, was a veritable treasure trove of reading. Gretel had pored over several of the tomes, and even taken several upstairs to read by candlelight. These books were not only the printed books of learning she was familiar with thanks to the old merchant. Here were diagrams of the human body, maps, descriptions of places she had never heard of – there seemed no limit to the knowledge Esther's library held, and the witch was happy to discuss whatever Gretel read. Perhaps most thrilling of all were those filled with Esther's own spidery handwriting, accompanied by intriguing recipes and sketches. *Spells*, Gretel had thought, and a mixture of excitement and fear had swirled inside her. She would spend all day in this room in a heartbeat.

Now, Gretel put down the knife. Esther kept teasing her about the boys' fates. Another test, perhaps.

"So what do you do with them?"

"Take a guess," said Esther.

Gretel thought back to the mysterious visitor who had knocked at the door the very first time she had been in the cottage – the woman in breeches, and the small cart she had left at the top of Esther's path. Esther had instructed Gretel to hand over a wooden crate containing glass jars. The liquid inside them was deep red. The colour of blood. Evidently, Esther and the woman had some pre-existing arrangement, for they had exchanged no words, only a pouch of gold. After the mysterious woman had left, Esther had counted the coins, nodded as though it was satisfactory, then shuffled away, presumably to hide the money.

That rumour is true, then, Gretel had thought. The witch was sitting on a pile of gold. How she obtained it ... well, that was the question.

Esther was waiting, expectant. Gretel wiped her palms on her apron.

"You've said you don't eat them," she said. "So perhaps you sell them, to feed other people?"

"Aha! Now you are using your brain."

"You cannot set foot in Westerleen, so you must do any trading in the towns and villages on the other side of the forest. I assume you do not steal their boys, or else they would never welcome you."

"Towns you have never visited." Esther leaned forwards. "Would you like to go there, next time I do? See what life is like outside of your dreary little village? There, you will understand exactly what my trade is. Why I care not for the lives of these foolish boys. Share my knowledge." She paused. "If you are not afraid of becoming a witch too, that is."

Gretel adjusted the collar of her gown, a fine dark blue one that

Esther had given her the day before. It felt wrong to feel excited about the prospect of exploring new places with Esther. Yet hadn't Mother once told her that people called any old woman who spoke her mind and didn't do as she was told a witch? So perhaps it wasn't such a bad thing. There could be different kinds of witches, couldn't there? Esther's knowledge did not need to be used for ill. She did not have to become Esther.

And Gretel very much wanted to know what the red liquid that went into those little bottles was. "Why do you not take girls?"

"I told you, the first time we spoke. When we came to our little agreement. Men cannot be trusted. It is always a bad idea to let them into your heart. Kindness is weakness. Fools and bullies, the lot of them."

Gretel thought of Jakob. He didn't seem like a fool or bully. He would be the first to die, she thought. Jakob was naturally slight, but much better-fed than Hansel. Unless she could help him, as she had promised.

"I'd better get back to cooking," she muttered.

Esther nodded. "I want those boys' plates empty and bellies full. Once they've eaten, I shall inspect them. Nice and fat, that's what we need."

Gretel suppressed a shudder. She had witnessed Esther

"inspecting" Hansel earlier; prodding and squeezing his fingers through a crack in the door. She rose to check the pot already simmering by the fireplace. Esther had instructed her to toss the chicken carcass into the liquid, so every sliver of meat and fat infused the stew. It looked ready, so Gretel heaved the pot to the table and picked out the bones and gristle. She thought of the bones she had uncovered in Esther's garden. Human bones, tossed into the dirt as though the fact that they had once belonged to a loved child meant nothing...

Gretel went still. Bones. Chicken bones. Human bones. She flexed her finger. The bone inside couldn't be that long. Very like this chicken one...

Perhaps she could buy Jakob – and Hansel – more time. She hesitated. Esther was sharing her home, her food and her knowledge – doing more for Gretel than anyone else had in years – and she, Gretel, was about to deceive her.

Before Gretel could think too much about it, she turned her back to the witch, snapped off two chicken bones and slipped them into the pocket of her apron.

After delivering the stew – and the chicken bones – to the boys, Gretel joined Esther outside the cottage, carrying a basket. Frost dusted the grass and earth, and faint mist drifted around them.

"Listen," said Esther, raising a finger to her lips.

The only sounds were small ones. Branches creaking in the breeze, faint, faraway movement, Esther's breathing. Gretel was about to ask what she was supposed to hear, then realized that was Esther's point. There was no one but them for miles. No jeering village boys or tired, fussy housewives or men's boots marching around.

A curious sense of peace settled on Gretel. Esther nodded, a knowing expression in her eyes. Leaning heavily on her stick, she shuffled from the cottage path and into the trees.

"It has been a while since I did this," she muttered. "You never lose the knack, though. Here. Know what those are?"

She nudged the thicket with her foot, revealing clumps of mushrooms. How she had known they were there, Gretel had no idea.

"Should I pick them?"

"Yes, but use the cloth. They're poisonous. The green tinge on the underside gives it away. If they leave even the smallest trace on your skin, you can forget cooking stew ever again."

With great care, Gretel collected the mushrooms, keeping them securely in the cloth Esther handed her. Esther continued on, still talking. "And the bark of these trees, that can be as nice or nasty as you like. Blend with some of the dried berries I keep inside, dilute with water, and murmur a few special witchy words, and that gives us the potion I used to lull your brother asleep. Just a drop into the gingerbread mix is enough to knock a person out for hours."

"Witchy words?"

Esther laughed. "Magic, spells, witchy words. They are all the same. The potion won't come alive without it."

As so often with Esther, Gretel couldn't decide whether she was being serious or not. She extracted the last mushroom and put it carefully in the basket. Esther led her deeper into the trees. The witch did not follow a path but seemed to know instinctively where to go. Was that familiarity, or some kind of arcane sense?

Esther stopped by what looked to be a collection of dirty glass bottles hanging by the trees, rope looped around the necks. She sniffed the top of one.

"Exhausted. As I thought."

Esther reached into her robe. Out came two little pouches Gretel recognized. The evening before, she had read aloud a recipe from one of Esther's handwritten books whilst the witch busied herself rubbing dried herbs together, then sprinkling the mixture with droplets from some of the bottles stored in the cupboard in the library. Its smell was an extraordinary mix of bitter and sweet, quite unlike anything Gretel was familiar with. Esther refused to be any more specific than to say she was making a "potion".

Sensing that Esther was waiting for her to ask, Gretel said, "So what are the bottles for?"

"I trap forest insects in them. What we made last night radiates a scent that is irresistible to them. It is also toxic. When we return tomorrow, with any luck, these jars will be brimming with bugs and beetles."

Gretel pulled a face. "What benefit is that?"

"Everything has its use, Gretel," chided Esther. "I have made a study of everything in this forest, from the tiniest ant to the tallest tree. My cottage's defences are growing weak. We need the blood from one particular bug to cast the spell that keeps them strong."

By "defences", Esther must be referring to the cottage remaining hidden to adults. So that really was a spell. Gretel had always wondered.

"How did you discover these things?"

Esther shrugged. "I am a witch. It is my business to discover things."

"Are all the spells in the books yours? Do you know other witches?"

Esther raised her eyebrows. "Careful, Gretel. Don't sound too enthusiastic. You never know who is listening."

Gretel spun round, half-expecting to see hunters bearing down on them. Of course, there was no one.

"Just keeping you on your toes," Esther smiled, but her expression wasn't a nice one. "Don't get too comfortable. Now, let's get to work."

They spent a while longer in the forest before Esther tired. The witch showed Gretel the animal traps and where to sprinkle one of her enticement potions to lure deer and bears to their doom.

"I prefer not to kill them," she said. "They don't trouble me, but sometimes needs must."

The next day, the hanging bottles were crammed with all kinds of insects. Gretel watched in fascination as Esther extracted the bugs and laid them out on the kitchen table, reeling off what each could be used for, though a few times she paused and frowned, muttering that her memory was not what it was. What must it feel like to have so much knowledge, but to have your body letting you down? Gretel drew up a chair of the right height so Esther could sit in comfort. The witch did not acknowledge the action, but Gretel spotted her smile.

When the bugs and beetles were ready, Gretel fetched another of Esther's spell books. She read the instructions aloud as Esther ground some eight-legged bugs Gretel did not know the name for into a disgusting-smelling paste. Esther opened others up with small, slightly rusted tongs – the kind that Gretel imagined a doctor might use. She began extracting specific parts of their innards and dropping them into a jar, but after fumbling three, Esther passed the task to Gretel.

"Can't do anything that precise any more," she grumbled. "One day I'll discover a spell to heal my wretched eyes. Be delicate now, Gretel, delicate."

The task was fiddly, but Gretel soon got the measure of it. There was something peculiarly satisfying about seeing the small jar fill. Gretel had been worried she wouldn't have the stomach for such work but found she didn't mind it at all. It was fascinating that such little things could be so powerful, combined with the other ingredients and a few murmured words. If Gretel had needed proof that Esther's powers worked, it was right here.

Powers that, perhaps, one day might be Gretel's, too.

Esther would not let her chant the spell as she boiled the insects and added droplets from her potion collection, though she relied on Gretel to read out what to say.

"There, it is done," she said after a few minutes. "Clear up, and we'll eat. Witchcraft is hungry work."

Soon they were sitting by the fire, enjoying steaming herbal teas and slabs of a rich, fruity cake Gretel had made from one of Esther's recipes the day before. Their silence was a companionable one. It was only as she swallowed the last mouthful that Gretel remembered Westerleen, and how cake like this was but a distant memory there. The crumbs turned dry and scratchy in her throat and she coughed.

"Oh, dear, dear," Esther patted her on the back. The witch's touch burned through her gown – one of the gowns that had once been Esther's. Gretel just about managed not to pull away. "Something wrong, or did you gobble that down too quickly?"

"I was thinking of Westerleen and the scarcity of food," Gretel admitted. "The villagers say crops do not grow because you cursed the fields." She hesitated. "Is that true?"

Esther's expression turned stony. Her eyes bored into Gretel, and Gretel shrank back a little. Suddenly she looked every inch the wicked witch. "You think I have that power?"

Gretel thought of the cottage shrouded in spells, the irresistible gingerbread and the traps that lured animals and insects. All impossibilities, and yet she had seen them with her own eyes.

"Yes," she whispered.

"Then that is your answer." The witch's voice was chilly. "I can do anything I like, Gretel. To anyone."

"Then why not use your powers for good?" Gretel asked boldly.

"Who do you think decides what is good and bad? The stupid men who scorned me, that's who. I do as I please." Esther tossed the dregs of her tea on the fire. It made a hissing sound. In that moment, Gretel could picture her as a younger woman – hard, bitter and teeming with anger. "There is no such thing as a good witch. You might think you can use powers to help people. You might try, and people might be grateful at first. Then they turn. They are not comfortable with power. They see it as a threat. I helped a family once, in Westerleen – a sick child. I knew that their old cures would not work and I knew what would. I thought they would be grateful – instead they turned on me. Mocked me. Spread word that I was dangerous, and to be avoided. The menfolk were especially vocal, and the women followed their lead. When my drunken fool of a husband burned down our house, they said I had cast a spell." Her voice dripped with scorn. "Witches do not hide in forests and mountains and caves because they are evil. They hide because of other people. That is the sacrifice you made when you came to me. Our powers give us freedom, but they take our freedom too. Do not talk of doing good again."

Gretel collected the plates and cups and took them to be washed without a word.

"Did something happen?" asked Jakob, when she crept down to see him later. He looked concerned. Concerned for *her*. Gretel wasn't used to being cared about. Jakob was the one in the dire predicament. The last couple of days, he'd picked up a cough, no doubt from the cold and wet. Perhaps she could smuggle down a healing potion...

"No," she said. "Why would it have done?"

"You did not come to speak to me yesterday."

With a start, Gretel realized she hadn't. The fresh air had tired her out, and her mind had been so full of Esther's magic, and whether the jars would fill with bugs, and miraculous spell books, that seeing Jakob had slipped her mind. Normally she looked forward to their chats.

"I'm sorry," she said.

"You don't owe me conversation." But Gretel knew he had kept awake waiting for her to come, and she felt guilty. So she changed the conversation and described going out into the forest and how quiet and peaceful it was outside.

"I will not forget to come and see you a second time," she

finished. "I am the one who has freedom, and I should be more generous."

Jakob pulled a face. "Freedom? Is that how you see it?"

"I am perfectly free," retorted Gretel. "I can go where I please. Read a whole library of books. Walk in the forest. I am not judged here. Esther even goes to markets sometimes. Not Westerleen, to the other side of the forest."

"Maybe, but she could turn on you at any point – as she keeps making clear." He stopped, coughing, then carried on. "You might not be in the danger Hansel and I are in, but you are not safe, are you?"

"You would say that. You want me to spring you from this cell and run back to Westerleen. I'm never going back there. Never."

As soon as the words were out, Gretel wanted to unsay them. Jakob stared at her. There were grey rings around his eyes, and for a moment he looked angry. Then his shoulders slumped. In a flat voice, he said, "You aren't going to save me, are you?"

"I didn't say that. I still want to get you out. But – but I think I want to stay. Maybe that sounds wrong to you, but you have to understand, there was so much I couldn't do at home that I can do here. The knowledge Esther has is incredible. My mind is open rather than narrow. It makes me feel bold and daring."

"Would you rather be here than at the university one day?"

"Don't be stupid," she snapped. "This isn't some debate you are having with your tutor. This is real life. My life."

"I'm not being stupid. I'm reminding you of what you told me you wanted."

Gretel turned away, taking deep breaths. "You don't know what it's like."

"What does Hansel think?"

Gretel recoiled, stung. Jakob frowned.

"You do speak to him, don't you?"

She dusted down her gown, not looking Jakob's way. "I should go."

She took the candle and hurried upstairs. By Hansel's cell she lingered. Jakob's question had made her uncomfortable. Gretel did her best not to speak to Hansel at all. She barely met his eyes when she delivered food. Hansel made it easy for her to ignore him. Since his capture, he had retreated in on himself and sat hugging his knees to his chest in the corner.

"No one has escaped the witch and I won't be any different," he'd muttered the one time she had asked him how he was. "I don't know why she keeps me here. I'd rather she just end it."

"Hansel, do you hold out the chicken bone when the witch comes?" Gretel had asked. He had only shrugged.

Hansel's silence suited her. It allowed Gretel to keep him at a distance, pretend he was a nameless boy who meant nothing to her, not her twin brother, who – even in the moment when she had made that desperate decision – she knew did not deserve the fate awaiting him.

Gretel swallowed. She hesitated. Then she turned and walked away from her brother's cell.

NOW

A LETTER FROM HOME

A Month After the Return

It took two weeks for Hansel's reply to arrive. He had dictated a few lines.

"*All well in Westerleen. Lord Fabian has sent us aid and we think we will weather winter. Hopefully there will be a better harvest now the witch is dead. Everyone talks of you. Father and I manage. See little of Ilse except when we eat. She is quiet, always at home, and only really speaks to me. Cristoph to marry Hilde Weber. Hope hands healed. Brida says hello. You are missed."*

Gretel raised her hands, inspecting the shiny, smooth scars on them. How funny of Hansel to remember the burns. Once the blisters had calmed, Gretel had barely given them a second thought.

She took herself for a walk to clear her head and muse over Hansel's letter. She was not permitted to wander the town unaccompanied – a rule she found ridiculous, when in Westerleen she had done so much alone – so she took to the manor house's gardens. They were starting to show welcome early signs of spring.

Gretel perched on a tree stump at the entrance that led to the stables and read the letter again. So Cristoph had moved on. That was good. Hopefully he had not shared the story about Gretel creeping into the forest with anyone who mattered. Did Hansel really miss her? It was hard to believe, but her brother wasn't a liar. So he must mean it. Brida did, no doubt. When she was better settled, she must see what she could do for Brida. She was too bright to be dulled by Westerleen and its mud.

A clattering sound made her jump. A barrel rolled at the mouth of the stable block. Running footsteps faded away.

Gretel was at the doorway in an instant, but whoever had been there was gone.

Had they been spying on her?

All kinds of wild thoughts ran through Gretel's mind. Then, her sense returned and she calmed down. No one was spying on her. It was a ridiculous thought. The footsteps had probably belonged to a servant. She was just jumpy because of Hansel's letter – which was silly, because it only contained good news. It seemed that Ilse was not causing trouble. That did bother Gretel a little, though. It was unlike Ilse to be quiet. Especially after all that talk of revenge. And the way her father had acted when she'd left Westerleen made her anxious. She doubted he'd tell anyone leaving the twins had been her suggestion – he had his pride – but all the same...

What if Ilse got the truth out of him somehow?

Gretel told herself not to fret. No one would listen to Ilse. She couldn't harm Gretel any more.

She folded Hansel's letter and reassured herself that Westerleen was well and truly in the past. Yet she couldn't fully silence the inner voice that whispered, *what if it isn't?*

THEN

EASTOWN MARKET

Ten Days After the Second Abandonment
and Four Days Before the Return

On the tenth day since Hansel had been captured, Esther announced, "Today, Gretel, we are going on a trip."

Gretel glanced up from where she was leafing through one of Esther's history books. Her head felt heavy this morning. She'd had another fascinating session in the forest yesterday, inspecting animal and insect snares, then mixing potions with Esther. The rest of the day she had spent reading.

It had been near-impossible to keep her eyes open when night fell, but she had made it to the cellar to see Jakob. Last night he had told her a story. While he had lived in Levalliers City, he had been caught attempting to sneak out of the house after nightfall to explore the streets by night. His tutor – a liberal-minded man who Jakob had liked – had been dismissed, and Jakob had relocated and been strictly supervised by his parents ever since.

"Where are we going?" she asked Esther now.

"You'll see."

The trip was surely tied to the fates of the boys. Gretel was a little surprised Esther was revealing this so soon. Sharing spells and forest lore was one thing, but this felt like a big secret, one that might change everything. Did that mean Esther now trusted her?

Gretel finished her chapter and made herself ready. A rap came from the front door. Outside was someone Gretel recognized: the woman she had given Esther's jars to what felt like a lifetime ago. There was another basket to go today, too. Gretel arranged it in the woman's cart, which was full of crates containing jars, food and clothes. They must be going to a market.

When Gretel and Esther were seated in the cart – which took a while, with Gretel and the woman helping Esther get comfortable – they set off. The woman drove the cart and it was a bumpy ride, for the forest path was not smooth. By the time the trees began to thin, Gretel was feeling nauseous. The track widened, and before too long the horse was clip-clopping along a road in much better condition to that which passed through Westerleen. Farmed fields and the odd cottage fleeted by, and the few people they passed offered greetings.

The world beyond Westerleen, thought Gretel, and a tingle ran up her spine. Had any of the children abandoned in the forest over the years found their way here?

Some time later, they reached a small town called Eastown. Gretel had heard the name before but little else; it was not governed by Lord Fabian, whose land was mostly in the other direction, and no one from Westerleen risked the uncertain journey through the forest to visit.

The cart came to a halt in Eastown's market square. Gretel leapt down, swinging her numb legs to get the feeling back into them. A glance told her that this place was considerably larger and more prosperous than Westerleen, with well-kept houses, proper shops and even water pumps.

"Help me out," Esther ordered. As Gretel took Esther's hands, two women passed by. They stopped and wished Esther a cheery good morning, inquiring about her health. Gretel's eyes popped. Didn't they recognize her as a witch? But as more townsfolk greeted Esther in the same way, Gretel began to realize that here, Esther was someone who commanded respect.

Nearby, the silent woman who had driven the cart was unloading Esther's jars on to a stall. The market was not fully open yet, but already a small crowd was growing. Gretel glanced at Esther, but she was busy chatting to someone.

"What are these?" she asked a woman at the back of the small crowd.

"Esther's tonics." When Gretel looked blank, the woman said, "They give strength and good health and youth." The woman laughed. "I'd love to know how she brews them, but it is an ancient herbal recipe and Esther guards it closely. I used to not believe they worked, but they really do. We are so rarely ill now, and I haven't noticed a new wrinkle in years. Esther really is wonderful."

"Isn't Esther a witch?" Gretel could not help but ask. The woman laughed again.

"How could anyone believe kind old Esther a witch? She is a wise woman."

In Westerleen those were one and the same, but perhaps in

Eastown attitudes were more forward-thinking. Gretel had spied several women working in shops from the cart, and there were no girls other than small ones on the streets. Perhaps this was one of the places Jakob had mentioned, where both boys and girls were educated.

If I had grown up here, people might not have mocked me, she thought, feeling a little heady. *I might even have been encouraged.*

"Gretel!" Esther shouted, and Gretel hastened over to help.

More and more jars exchanged hands. Gretel's discomfort grew. Perhaps she was wrong to think that today's trip was linked to the fate of Esther's prisoners. Yet she couldn't shake off the sense that there was something the witch was holding back

"Just your tonics today, Esther?" A beaming mother with two young children enquired. Both were boys.

Esther smiled graciously. "Next time, I promise you pies."

Pies? The word was a bolt through Gretel's heart. The boys' mother expressed delight and said she would get to the market early. Esther caught Gretel watching.

"This is my trade, Gretel." She sounded smug. "See how the tonics fly into their hands? They love me here – have done for years – and I live a comfortable life because of it. When everything is sold, we shall shop for food."

The words stuck in Gretel's mouth, but she had to say them. "What's in the pies, Esther?"

"Ah, my miraculous pies." That awful smile spread across Esther's face. "They are very popular when I am able to make them. Full of hearty goodness, baked with love from Esther's nourishing recipes. Soon we shall have plenty to sell."

Gretel suddenly feared she was going to be sick, right here in the middle of the bustling square. Esther smacked her shoulder.

"Poor Gretel. Has something disagreed with you?"

"You … cook the boys," Gretel whispered. "You make them into pies. To sell to people who have no idea what they are eating."

"The tonics come from the boys, too." Esther's tone was breezy, as though they were two housewives discussing the best way to flavour chicken. "I collect their blood and infuse it into my herbal brew, much like I have shown you already. Nothing like the blood of healthy lads to give strength and vigour. Works like magic."

She winked. Gretel could barely bring herself to look at Esther. All she could see, in her head, were the faces of those poor missing boys. Hansel's face … and Jakob's. Their bodies in pies; blood in tonics. Killed to line the witch's pockets. Innocent people eating them, believing the most terrible of lies.

For a wild moment, Gretel wanted to shout out the truth, tell these people that Esther was tricking them. But that would be foolish, and dangerous. Younger and stronger she might be, but Gretel was no match for the witch's dark magic. How could she have believed Esther anything other than evil?

I've been a fool, she thought. *I was desperate and saw what I wanted to see, not what was there.*

With enormous effort, Gretel managed to keep her voice calm. "But these are people's lives, Esther. My own people."

"Westerleen deserves all the grief I inflict on it, and more." Esther's voice was hard and bitter. "I've told you before, the land is full of worthless, arrogant boys who grow up to become useless, bullying men. I remove a few before they reach that point, that is all."

Distorted and twisted though it was, Esther was right there. The nastier Westerleen boys had sneered at Gretel, and the others had followed like sheep. Even Cristoph was a bully, though he feigned righteousness.

"Take your brother," continued Esther. "As you told me, a boy who shuts his eyes to the injustice around him. Then there is the rich boy, a tyrant in the making. It is his father's governance that has kept Westerleen and other such villages backwards. So I feel no pity. It is a business. You have to be ruthless to thrive in this sorry life. You see that, don't you?"

You don't have to kill innocent children, thought Gretel. She thought of Hansel, who was kind and gentle and no bully. Jakob, with his progressive ideas, was no tyrant.

"Gretel!" snapped Esther. "I said, you see that, don't you?"

There was a dangerous note in the witch's voice. Gretel forced herself to look Esther directly in the eyes. "I want to learn from you. I think I've shown that."

There was a long pause. Then, Esther patted Gretel on the shoulder. Her softer side was back. "I knew from the moment you found your way to my cottage that we were kindred spirits." She paused. "I see so much of myself in you."

Someone came to speak to Esther, and the witch turned away.

Gretel leaned against the side of the cart, fighting the sick feeling in her belly. Her attention was drawn by a nearby merchant. He had a round, bald head and was staring at her, frowning. In an instant Gretel recognized him as the cloth trader who often visited Westerleen. She had haggled with him only two weeks ago for cloth intended to become part of her wedding dress. No doubt he was wondering why on earth a Westerleen girl was here, with the wicked witch, no less!

Gretel turned her back quickly. It didn't matter. The merchant would forget her before he returned to Westerleen. He wasn't important. The nausea in the pit of her stomach grew.

The truth was that Gretel had known, all along, what Esther was. She had just chosen not to see it. And now that she had, the question was – what would she do now?

That night, Gretel told Jakob about the trip to Eastown. He listened in silence as she told him about the pies and the tonics and the crowds of cheerful townsfolk. When she was done, she stared into the darkness.

"I need to get you and Hansel out as soon as possible," she whispered.

"That's not enough," said Jakob. "We need to stop her."

Gretel was silent. She pressed the palm of her head to her forehead. Jakob was right, she knew that. Esther was evil. But Esther had not been born that way.

"You admire her, don't you?" said Jakob curiously. "Still, after all you've discovered."

"I-I have some sympathy for her, that's all." Gretel floundered for the words. "Esther built her life from nothing. It was others who drove her to this. She told me her story."

"No one forced her to kill people."

Gretel bit her lip. "It is not that simple."

Jakob's voice hardened. "Isn't it?" He leaned forward, closer to the bars. "Do you still want to stay here, Gretel? Even after what you saw today, knowing that she will kill me and your brother – you want to stay?"

Did she? Gretel didn't answer immediately.

A life on her own terms. That was what she wanted. Was that what Esther had?

Silence spread across the cellar, interrupted only by the drip of water from the corner and the scuttle of rats.

Gretel thought of the market; the potions, the talk of pies. The missing boys and grieving families.

There was only one answer to Jakob's question.

Gretel heaved a sigh and straightened.

"No," she said. "I don't want to stay. I would spend my life hiding. A witch. Because that is the only option for a woman who does not want to play by the rules. I want a life *within* the rules."

"Are you sure?"

"Yes. I'm sure."

Jakob nodded. He waited, watching her.

Gretel exhaled and looked at Jakob properly for the first time.

"If I were to … do something about Esther … I would receive a reward. Is that correct?"

"Ah, yes," he said, in a flat voice. "My father does like to reward people."

"What do you mean?"

Jakob shifted on the hard floor. The energy he'd had about him when they'd first spoken had dwindled in the last couple of days, and his cough was worse. Gretel wished she could reach inside and hug him.

"Jakob," she said. "What aren't you telling me?"

There was a long pause. Then Jakob looked up. "Father will never reward you."

His words rippled through Gretel like a stone skimming water. "But he is wealthy," she said. "Esther is regarded as a monster and I would slay her. Monster slayers get rewarded."

"Yes, but you won't." Quietly, Jakob said, "Gretel, my father won't reward a girl. I told you he would before because … well, I needed to persuade you, but … you won't see a penny of the reward. Any money will go to the man responsible for you."

"This cannot be true."

"Take it from someone who knows. Perhaps you heard of the man who disposed of the river creatures near Ennisport? I happen to know that his wife was the one who speared them. Yet no one is talking about her. Father was grateful, yes, but she could not claim the reward herself. Stories spread, and now everyone thinks her husband is the hero."

Surely not, Gretel thought dully. Lord Fabian was a civilized, educated man – surely he wouldn't participate in such lies? And yet Gretel thought back to three years ago, when she and Hansel had emerged from the woods. Albrect and the other Westerleen men had assumed Hansel to be the one who laid the pebble trail the first time the twins had been abandoned. How many other women and girls had their ideas and actions stolen from them by boys and men?

Gretel stared at Jakob, her mouth dry. Would it be worth returning to the world outside Esther's cottage if there was no reward on the other side? Within days – hours, even – she would be back living the dismal life that had driven her here. Cooking, cleaning, marriage to Cristoph – or worse, to Heinrich Mulch. No books, no travel, nothing.

I cannot do it! she thought.

Yet she knew she could not stay, either. She could not let Esther kill more boys.

"Gretel, listen." Jacob pressed his face to the bars. "I have another idea. One that better protects you and might even help you to one day get to the university. It involves you trusting me, just like I've been trusting you, but that seems fair enough, doesn't it?"

Gretel considered him. "What is your idea, then?" she asked.

"It is more of a promise..." And Jakob explained.

NOW

THE SPRING FESTIVAL

Two Months After the Return

The Spring Festival came two months after Gretel had left Westerleen. There would be singing and dancing for several days, and a succession of merchant folk from all the villages in the region would be passing through the manor house to discuss trading during the seasons ahead with Lord Fabian.

Celebrations would also be held in Westerleen. Gretel's fondest memories of her village came from the week of the Spring Festival.

For seven days, petty grievances and hardships faded away. Everything was smiles and laughter. Gretel had always loved how – almost overnight – the air lightened, the bite of winter chill died and flower scents mingled with the mud. She now felt something she could never have imagined: homesick.

"What are you thinking?" Jakob asked her one day when they were seated on the grass at the end of Lord Fabian's gardens, Ottillie a discrete distance away sewing with a servant.

"About home," Gretel said, chin on hand. "At this time of year, the blossom comes out and the birds wake me with their song. Westerleen feels a completely different place. Hopeful, somehow. And the river is so clear."

Jakob watched her for a moment. "Why don't we go to Westerleen, then? There is nothing to stop us taking the carriage there."

Gretel froze. "I cannot."

"Why not? If you are worried about it being awkward, it needn't be. You saved them. They'll be delighted to see you."

"My father and stepmother won't be."

"Then we won't speak to them."

Jakob spoke as though it was simple. He didn't understand the threat Gretel still felt hanging over her – but then, how could he. "I still think it is a bad idea," she said.

"You just told me you were homesick." He nudged her foot with his. "It would give me a chance to see your village at its best, rather than full of mud."

Gretel cast around for an excuse. "Won't your father need you here?"

Jakob rolled his eyes. "Since when has Father ever needed me? As long as I greet his guests, he won't even notice. You could see Hansel. You keep fretting about him."

It was true that Hansel had been on Gretel's mind. He hadn't yet replied to her second letter.

Gretel hesitated. Jakob noticed.

"Come on," he said. "I want to see these celebrations you told me about."

"They will be a poor showing compared to what you are used to."

Jakob brushed her hand with his. "Gretel, I want to spend the day with you, without being watched by my parents or their servants." He gave her a grin. "Please?"

Gretel found herself smiling back. After all, why shouldn't she go? Westerleen was still her home village. Cristoph was no longer a threat, promised as he was to Hilde Weber. Ilse couldn't do anything to her now. Most likely, the villagers would welcome her, and they would spend a pleasant few hours watching singers and maybe dancing. She could also see how Brida was. Gretel thought of the little girl often. She had sent her a present with the same messenger who had delivered the letter to Hansel – a fine and especially warm cloak which had been one of Ottillie's – but she did not know if it had been received safely. And Esther's cottage would have been searched by now – it might be useful to discover what had been found.

"All right," she said reluctantly. "But just for the festival."

The beaming smile Jakob gave her made Gretel feel like it was the right decision. He was smiling a lot these days, Gretel had noticed. So, it appeared, was she. Whenever she caught a glimpse of herself in a mirror, or reflection in water, her lips were upturned.

She found she liked the idea of spending the day with him too.

The day Gretel and Jakob planned to visit Westerleen dawned and, as Gretel had somehow known it would, the sun shone brightly. The manor was a blaze of colour and full of beautifully dressed people. Attired in a dusky pink gown – a colour that suited her – she drifted round the garden, watching merchants and farmers arrive. From the snatches of conversation she overheard, everyone was optimistic for a better year.

"After every dark winter comes a bright spring," she heard a wine merchant saying earnestly.

As well as the guests, Gretel's eyes were on Jakob, who moved from group to group, offering greetings and polite questions and introductions. He did it seamlessly, despite his complaints about detesting such functions. *He is far less difficult than people accuse him of being,* she thought, and the protective anger she felt surprised her.

Jakob found her later, after Lord Fabian had called the most important merchants and farmers into the great hall. "I have done my duty, now let's escape," he said. "It is still early, and we will have plenty of time in Westerleen. You look very nice, by the way."

"Oh. Thank you." Gretel smoothed down her dress, feeling suddenly self-conscious. "Wouldn't you rather enjoy the festival here with your friends? There is no need to feel obliged to entertain me. Westerleen's festival is modest—"

"I do not feel remotely obliged. There is no one else I would rather spend the day with." As always, he offered her his arm. Gretel no longer minded this as she once had. As they walked to the carriage, she was very aware of the contact between her arm and his, in a way she would not have been weeks ago.

It took a little while to navigate the horse and carriage through the teeming streets, but once they cleared the town, the journey passed quickly. Jakob was in one of his high-spirited moods and made Gretel laugh with outrageous stories from the city. Yet as they neared the edges of Westerleen, her mood blackened. It felt airless in the carriage.

The carriage drew up by The Green Gate, where there were stables for the horses to be fed and watered. Would there be a crowd? Yes, of course there would. *The carriage will have been spotted some minutes ago*, Gretel thought, *and speculation will no doubt already be flying around that his lordship is returning.*

"This is a bad idea," she whispered. "We shouldn't have come."

Jakob's hand found hers, and squeezed. "Don't worry, Gretel," he murmured. "I understand why you're nervous, but I'm sure it will be fine. We can leave whenever you want."

The guard who'd accompanied them opened the door to excited chattering. As she swung herself out, someone cried, "It is Gretel!" Her name rippled through the growing crowd. Gretel risked a glance upwards. Smiles – they were happy to see her.

Something hurled itself at Gretel, temporarily winding her. It clung on, before peeling off to reveal a delighted looking Brida.

"What are you doing here?" she cried. "No one told me you were coming."

"No one knew. Oh, you are wearing the cloak I sent!"

Brida gave her a twirl. "I never take it off. Everyone is jealous I look so fine. It is a little warm today, but I don't care." She beckoned Gretel closer, then whispered, "I've kept the book safe, exactly as you wanted! I might have found someone to help me learn to read it, only that's a secret."

"Gretel." It was Albrect, a little out of breath, presumably from having hurried over from the meadow where the minstrels were. "This is a pleasant surprise. It is good to see you."

He bowed – actually bowed. Gretel's eyes went big. Jakob hid his laughter while smoothly saying, "Gretel told me about your festivities, and we thought we would join. I apologize for not sending word. Inside the carriage are crates of iced biscuits and candied nuts. Please could you see that they are taken to the meadow for all to share?"

Albrect clapped his hands, delighted, and called for some boys to carry the crates. *That was a nice gesture*, Gretel thought, glad Jakob had thought of it. More villagers thronged round them, all asking how she had been and expressing delight that she was here. Gretel's uncertainty and self-consciousness eased; everyone really was genuinely pleased to see her – but they were also too keen to enjoy themselves to linger.

As she and Jakob followed the trickle of villagers to the meadow, Gretel was able to take in her old home properly. Westerleen had transformed. Gone was the frost and the worst of the mud. In their place were early blooms, and the smell of a hog roast, and music. Perhaps it was her imagination, but the smiles were bigger and the laughter louder. This year, everyone could enjoy themselves without Esther's shadow hanging over them. She'd already heard murmurings of richer soil and more flowers blooming. Was that merely spring, or was it the result of Esther's dark magic lifting?

"Are we staying?" Jakob whispered into her ear.

Gretel smiled. "We're staying."

The afternoon whirled into early evening. They danced until their feet were throbbing, listened to live storytelling for the children and enjoyed vegetable-filled pastries. Thanks to Lord Fabian's aid, it appeared food, while not yet plentiful, was no longer such a scarcity.

Gretel's reunion with her family, too, was not as difficult as she had been expecting. Her father had little to say beyond pleasantries and soon disappeared, but Hansel held out his arms. Gretel was taken aback at first, but then leaned in to hug him.

"You look well," he said.

"So do you," Gretel said warmly. It was true. Her brother's skin had a healthy colour to it and he was wearing clothes she did not recognize – not fine, as such, but less worn than the tunics she had resented washing. The friends he was with were also better dressed than she had expected. "Are those new clothes?"

Hansel explained that shortly after Gretel had left, a search party had found Esther's cottage. "We found her gold. There was so much, Gretel, more than we'd ever imagined. Albrect distributed it equally between the men, as well as everything else in the cottage. It was so good to be able to buy new things. Even after we received aid, the rest of winter was hard but we managed to get by."

"What did they do with her books?"

"Those were burned."

Of course. Gretel felt a pang of sadness. All that knowledge – that power – gone, because the villagers were afraid.

Hansel pulled away; eyebrows quizzical. "Why have you come, Gretel? I didn't think you liked it here."

"I couldn't miss the festival, could I?" Gretel said. "I wanted to see you, too. How is everything at home? You did not say much in your letter."

"There is little to say. Father gets by, the same as ever, and Ilse … well…" He shrugged, smiling. "You know what Ilse is like."

"Oh yes," said Gretel wryly. "I do know what Ilse is like. Let me guess – pursed lips, hands on hips and long sighs?"

Hansel laughed, and Gretel grinned.

"That is Ilse, every day," he said. At Ilse's name, someone behind them made a disgusted noise and muttered a rude word. Gretel glanced back, wondering who had spoken. Instead, she caught sight of Cristoph over the far side of meadow. He was with Hilde Weber. She appeared to be listening attentively to something he was saying. Cristoph had his back to Gretel. It might be coincidence, but she had the feeling he had spotted her and intended to stay well away.

She turned back to Hansel. "Is Ilse here, then?"

"Not likely," said one of Hansel's friends, with a sneer. Hansel opened his mouth to say something, but then the minstrels started a merry tune and Jakob pulled Gretel towards the dancing, and she forgot about her brother.

As the skies became dusky, by silent agreement Gretel and Jakob headed to the river and stood at the spot where Gretel had so often dreamed, watching the water flicker and flow. Above them, birds cheeped. The trees had been silent the last time she had been here. There were other sounds too; the hush of breeze in the long grass, the creak of branches – and gentle snapping. Like someone treading on a twig.

Gretel went still. Her mind leaped to the time she had felt as though she was being watched in Lord Fabian's garden. Was someone there?

She glanced around, but the slope of the riverbank behind was too steep to see far. "Jakob, did you—"

"Did I what?"

"Never mind." She was being foolish. It was probably just a rabbit, or some other animal. "I enjoyed today. I'm so glad you persuaded me to come."

"Good," Jakob said. "I am glad I was able to enjoy it with you." His expression clouded over. "I think I underestimated how strange it would be for me."

"What do you mean?"

"This is the place where I almost died. I do not talk of it much, because, well, there seems little point, but..." He paused. "Days in that dark cell felt endless. Even knowing you were there, I was afraid. It will be a long time before I can forget that. Maybe never. I wish... I wish I could be as untroubled by it all as you clearly are."

Gretel hadn't known he felt that way. This time she was the one to squeeze his hand. Jakob blinked, glancing downwards. A beat passed. Then, he squeezed back.

"Things could have turned out differently, but they didn't." Gretel's words felt clumsy. "That is what you should focus on, not the fear. I did not realize it affected you so – you seemed flippant when you spoke of the cottage."

He shrugged. "Only because it makes it easier to deal with. I don't want to carry on pretending it doesn't trouble me … not with you, anyway. That would be a lie, and I don't like lying."

Gretel wished she could comfort him properly, but she was afraid of where this might go. "We need to forget about Esther and her cottage – both of us. If I can do anything to help, I will. I hate the idea of you hurting."

"You do help. Thinking about you keeps the worst of it from my mind." He cleared his throat. "I think about you quite a lot. And not just how I can help you fulfil your dreams."

His hand felt like fire in hers. Not the angry fire she had been so used to. Gretel let out a long breath. Suddenly, all she wanted in this moment was to be a girl, hand in hand with a boy, with so much to look forward to.

Not a girl hiding secrets.

"Maybe you shouldn't," she found herself saying. "This was not our agreement…"

He took her other hand. Gretel stopped.

"I cannot do this, Jakob."

"Cannot, or don't want to?" His voice was husky.

Cannot. Because of everything you don't know.

She inhaled the fresh river air. It was best she stopped this before it even began – however much she might want to see where it headed. Jakob's feelings would never last. Hadn't both Lord Fabian and Ottillie said he was restless? He'd tire of her before long. That would make things easier.

"I am sorry," she made herself say.

Jakob dropped her hands and stepped back. "No, I am sorry. I misunderstood. I won't stop helping you, though, don't worry about that."

He was withdrawing. He was hurt despite pretending not to be. Gretel could not bear it. She closed the gap between them, leaned forwards and brushed his lips with hers.

"You didn't misunderstand," she whispered. "I don't know why I said that. I think I'm scared."

"Don't be."

This time, Jakob kissed Gretel, drawing his arms around her. She experienced fleeting panic before happiness took her over. The kisses were tentative at first, with both Gretel and Jakob feeling this new experience out, then deeper and more confident. By the time they drew apart, Gretel was glowing.

He doesn't need to know, she told herself. *Not all lies are bad.*

Gretel would have liked to have lingered longer by the river but if they were to return to the manor, it was time to leave. They scaled the bank and, walking hand in hand, set off down the track that led back to the village. A flicker of movement caught Gretel's attention. This time she was sure she had seen someone.

"Who's there?" she cried.

A cloaked figure stepped out from the bushes and lowered their hood.

THEN

THE OVEN IS LIT

*Two Weeks After the Second Abandonment
and the Day of the Return*

Esther scowled as the door to Hansel's cell closed with a heavy clang. Two weeks into Gretel's stay in the cottage and the witch had awoken in a foul mood. Nothing was right. The porridge Gretel presented her with was lukewarm, the sun too bright and her joints stiff. And she was even less pleased now she had inspected her two prisoners.

"Are they eating the food you cook?" she demanded. "Your brother's fingers are as skinny as ever! I thought you said he ate like a horse, given the chance?"

Gretel kept a composed face, not that it mattered. If Esther still believed the chicken bones were fingers, she could hardly read Gretel's expression from half a room away. "The plates and bowls I take from the cells are clean. Some boys, I am told, remain skinny no matter what they eat."

"Both of them? What poor luck," Esther grumbled, shuffling into the kitchen. "One boy is for the oven this week, thin or fat. My customers clamour for pies, and I'll not disappoint them. I need to brew new potions, too."

So this was it, Gretel thought. It was happening.

She forced herself to sound indifferent. "Who will you choose?"

"It matters not. They're both too scrawny. The boy in the cellar, probably. He is troublesome. I'll pop a sleeping draught in his milk. We'll never get him in the oven otherwise."

"So that is what you do? Drug them, so they cannot fight back."

"You are stupid this morning, Gretel. Of course they are drugged. How else could I manage?" Esther stroked her chin. "Perhaps I'll choose your brother instead. His spirit seems broken.

He'll probably walk into the oven willingly. Poor boy, I think he has accepted his fate. What do you think, Gretel?"

Esther locked eyes with Gretel and in that moment, Gretel had the uncanny sense that the witch could see every single one of her doubts. It took all Gretel's nerve to shrug, as though they were discussing the price of potatoes.

"It matters not to me. If you want my opinion…" She hesitated, quickly thinking ahead. "I would take my brother. It is cruelty to keep him in the cell any longer."

Esther raised her eyebrows. "He is less well-fed. A few weeks more and he may yet fatten up."

"Perhaps. But he is bigger and broader than the lord's son."

Esther waved her hand, as though she could not be bothered discussing it any longer. "Very well. Your brother it is. In a few days, I shall fire up the oven."

Gretel went still. She was aware of everything. The soft bubbling from the stew on the stove. The rustle of leaves from the forest beyond. The creak of Esther's chair. *This is the moment,* she realized. She had made her decision. The more she waited, the more she questioned herself – and the worse her fears became.

Would she be brave enough, when the moment came?

I will soon find out.

Gretel counted to ten in her head. Then she said, "Why not now?"

Esther's eyebrows shot still higher. "Do you not want to give your brother a final few days, Gretel? That is unkind of you."

There she went, baiting her again. As though life – and death – was a game.

"You said it yourself," said Gretel. "My brother has given up."

"Well, then. Your wish is my command. I'll prepare that sleeping draught."

"Is that necessary?" Gretel said. She was amazed at how even her voice was. "Hansel will be meek. If his hands are bound, he can hardly fight back." Then, when Esther looked unconvinced, she said, "Please, Esther. This is a moment I will remember always. I would rather he was awake."

At that, Esther laughed, and the sound chilled Gretel. Sounding half-impressed, the witch said, "I did not realize you were quite so callous. I applaud you. Light the oven. Then you may collect him."

Wordlessly, Gretel went to the oven and busied herself clearing out yesterday's ash. Her hands shook. A few minutes later, flames roared beneath the grate. The horrible meaty smell that never truly went away filled the air. Gretel stood, wiping sweat from her forehead. Despite the ferocious heat, inside she was as ice.

"I will get Hansel." She looked at Esther, remembering their time in the forest and how, briefly, they had felt close. "It is time we said our final goodbye."

NOW

TRUTH OR LIES

Two Months After the Return

"Surprised to see me, Gretel?"

Gretel could only stare at her stepmother. She realized she had barely given Ilse a thought all afternoon – she had been far too wrapped up enjoying herself with Jakob.

"You have been spying on us." Gretel's mind leapt to the time she thought herself watched before. "Not just here, but at the manor house, too. How did you even get there?"

"Plenty of merchant wagons go between there and Westerleen. You are not the only one who can be resourceful. Were you really going to leave without at least saying hello, when we have so much to talk about?"

"Gretel," said Jakob, voice softly warning, a hand at her elbow. "You do not have to speak to her. The carriage is ready. We can leave."

Gretel shook her head, eyes locked on Ilse. "Why spy on me?"

Ilse folded her arms. Gretel noticed her hair was untidy, the bottom of her creased gown mud-flicked. "I wanted to see what you were up to. You upended my life with your lies, Gretel. I am dirt in Westerleen. No one will speak to me. They turn away when I approach. Your father looks through me. It is as though I am a ghost. Did you intend that, when you made your plans?"

"I don't know what you mean."

Ilse stepped closer. "Let's not pretend, Gretel. My congratulations, you pulled everything off impeccably. We have a lot in common, I think. Perhaps I should have been kinder to you."

Esther's words came to Gretel: *we are alike.* Why were these women – both outliers in their own way – so keen to see her in their image? Could she not be a person all of her own? "I am nothing like you – or the witch," she said fiercely. "You have no power over me any more."

Jakob spoke up. He'd stepped in front of Gretel, as though shielding her. "The promise was my idea, not Gretel's."

Ilse eyed him speculatively. "Tell me," she said. "Your conversations with my stepdaughter in the cottage. What were they about? I know you spoke, often. Hansel has said as much."

Hansel! What had he told Ilse? "I thought you said you were dirt and no one was talking to you."

"Your brother is the exception. He has a kind heart. Not something anyone could ever accuse you of having, Gretel."

"Kindness is weakness," whispered Gretel, aware she was parroting Esther. She saw Jakob frown.

"I asked a question." Ilse's eyes were on Jakob. Jakob hesitated.

Reluctantly, he said, "The university, mainly. Gretel was curious about it."

"Presumably you also plotted your escape?"

"Well, naturally." Jakob's eyes flickered to Gretel. "I encouraged Gretel to kill the witch. I am not proud of suggesting she take someone's life. It troubles me still, witch or no witch. But I needed to survive. I thought if I played up a possible reward, then Gretel would take it seriously."

"And later you told Gretel that your father would never reward a girl, which she did not believe but turned out to be true," said Ilse. Gretel went cold. Hansel couldn't have known all this – Ilse must have pieced it together from what he *had* said.

"It felt important to be honest…" Jakob trailed off. Ilse was wearing a look of amusement.

She is going to destroy me, thought Gretel, and felt sick to her stomach.

"Leave him alone, Ilse," Gretel said sharply. "We can talk in private. Jakob, can you go to the inn? I will meet you there when we're done."

Jakob hesitated. "I don't want to leave you—"

"Just go," Gretel said.

She and Ilse waited, in silence, until they were alone.

"You should thank me," Ilse said. "I could have ruined everything for you just now."

Gretel turned her back to the nearby trees. They reminded her too much of the forest. "I don't know what you mean."

"I know about the pebbles," said Ilse.

Gretel tried to channel some of Ilse's coldness, hoping it masked her fear. "You will need to be more specific."

"Three years ago, you used pebbles to guide you home. Then, two months ago, you used them to guide you to Esther."

Don't say anything, Gretel thought. Just let her talk. Find out what she knows.

"Cristoph was watching that day, you know. He said you entered the woods that morning with some kind of bundle and were seen returning that afternoon without it. I think you found the witch's cottage that morning all by yourself – you're a smart girl. And then you laid a trail so that you would find your way back again when you returned with Hansel."

Curse Cristoph, thought Gretel. Even though he was marrying another woman, still he wanted her ruined.

Ilse continued. "Hansel remembers little of being led into the trees by your father, but he does recall you telling Georg which way to go. You evidently had a destination in mind. Hansel is quite stupid, but he is not unobservant. You underestimated him."

The only thing I underestimated was your hatred of me, thought Gretel. She remained silent.

"That night in the forest was not the first time you had been to the witch's cottage," Ilse said. "You had been there the day before. Which puts a very different slant on everything."

In a low voice, Gretel said, "You have no proof."

"Haven't I? Hansel noticed the pebbles. So did your father. Who, by the way, is so scared of what you are capable of that he can no longer even utter your name." Ilse's lip twisted. "His weakness disgusts me. You manipulated him and he knows it, yet he will not speak up."

"Why would he? No one would ever believe that we would volunteer to go into the forest."

"Unfortunately. And thus, I remain your father's scapegoat. Well done, Gretel. Did you enjoy seeing me undone?"

"Yes," said Gretel.

Ilse smiled, and not in a nice way. "You wanted what Esther had, didn't you? Knowledge, power and money. I originally thought you desired to become her apprentice, but now I think it more likely that your closeness was an act, to fool the witch. You planned to kill her and come home a hero. As for Hansel…"

Ilse paused, frowning. For a moment Gretel's heart stopped completely. "Hansel was the perfect witness. You needed him to see you acting the hero, otherwise who would believe you? And when you discovered Jakob, well, that was even better. He was the perfect way to leave Westerleen. What girl wouldn't like the idea of becoming a lady? Much better than a witch. You've certainly been enjoying the manor house from what I have observed. Everything was planned."

Gretel reached out to steady herself, palm brushing tree bark.

So Ilse did not quite know everything. She had missed out the worst part.

She took a deep breath. "What do you want from me, Ilse?"

"I want my reputation back. I want you to confess that neither I nor your fool of a father abandoned you in the woods. I want you to tell everyone that you planned it yourself, because you had ideas beyond your station, because you wanted everyone to think you a hero – and you led your own brother into danger. You escaped with your lives – but barely. I want you to tell everyone how foolhardy and arrogant you were."

"No," cried Gretel. "I won't do that."

"I had a feeling that would be your response," said Ilse. She leaned close. "In that case then, I want money. Enough to set me up with a new life somewhere else. A comfortable life – the kind I expected when I married your father – with fine clothes, and a warm fire, and a full belly. Give me those things, and I will keep my mouth shut."

Gretel clenched her teeth. "You are blackmailing me."

"I am doing what I need to in order to get what I want, just as you did."

Gretel closed her eyes. In her mind's eye, she saw one of Jakob's polished chess pieces sliding towards her.

Checkmate.

"I will give you tonight to decide," said Ilse. "The money, or my reputation. Perfectly simple." Gretel hated how bright and breezy Ilse sounded – almost as though she was holding back laughter. "I will come to the manor tomorrow to hear your decision."

Ilse did not wait for Gretel's agreement. She strolled away, a spring in her step. Gretel slumped against the nearest tree, her hands over her face. Those wretched pebbles! They had saved her life but also damned her. Between them, Hansel, Cristoph and Ilse would be her undoing.

She could tell the truth. Or she could lie and spend her life paying off Ilse. That was what her decision boiled down to.

If she told the truth … she would be shunned. She would have to leave Westerleen. And the truth would inevitably follow her to Lord Fabian's house. The full truth. And Jakob would hear it.

She cared about what he thought. Very much, it turned out.

Gretel's chest constricted. Why hadn't she kept Jakob more distant? What a fool she'd been! Against all her better instincts, she had let down her guard. Not just in the cottage, but since – the fleeting moments snatched when they were unobserved, and the long evenings playing chess or discussing books. She wanted more days like today, when they could laugh and touch and be close to each other – and he wanted that too.

Kindness is weakness, Esther had said. Gretel didn't believe that. Jakob had been kind when it would have been easy not to be. That did not make him weak. But what else had Esther said? *It is always a bad idea to let men into your heart.* She might have been right about that.

How Esther would be laughing if she was here now.

If I tell the truth, I will lose him. It was a certainty; as day followed night. She would also lose Lord Fabian's already tenuous goodwill. She would be cast out, with nothing.

Or she could continue the lie and pay Ilse. Would money really settle things, though? Gretel had none of her own. It would have to come from Jakob. She had no idea how far his generosity stretched. What if Ilse ran into hard times? She would be back with more demands, a leech sucking Gretel's blood. That was inevitable too.

She would be using Jakob to further her deception.

"I am damned whatever I choose," whispered Gretel.

Jakob was pacing by the carriage. He hurried over when he saw her.

"What did she say?"

Gretel pressed a hand to her forehead. "I cannot talk now. I feel unwell. Please can we leave?"

"You will tell me everything later, though?"

She nodded, though she knew she wouldn't. Jakob opened the carriage door and she clambered inside. He joined her, sitting close.

"Gretel," he said quietly. "Know that, whatever your stepmother wants, I will help you. Just give me the word. Allies, remember?"

"Some day you will be tired of helping me." The words stuck in Gretel's throat. "Your life would be a lot simpler without taking on my troubles."

"Maybe, but it would also be a lot worse." His voice deepened. "I'll never tire of you, Gretel."

He put his arms around her. Gretel wanted to lean into him but instead she turned away as the carriage started up and gathered pace. She felt as though she wanted to bawl like a baby. It struck her that if there was no Ilse, there would be no threat... No. What was she thinking? Pushing the witch into the oven was different. Esther had killed all those boys and had been about to kill two more – including her brother. Any guilt Gretel felt about her death was fleeting. Ilse was cruel, and malicious, and manipulative, but not a monster. There was no flaming oven to push her into anyway.

So that left her with a simple decision that was anything but.

Truth, or lies.

THEN

ESTHER'S DEMISE

Two Weeks After the Second Abandonment
and the Day of the Return

Hansel did not look up when Gretel opened his cell. He was slumped in the corner, chin propped against his chest. Gretel crouched in front of him.

"Hansel."

He didn't answer. Gretel took his wrists and looped rope

around them. Only when she tightened and knotted it did Hansel's head snap up.

"What are you doing?"

"It is time."

Raw, unfiltered panic shot on to Hansel's face. He stared at her with wide eyes. Gretel had never hunted but she imagined this was the look the animals wore just before the kill, and it turned her insides to ice. She waited for him to protest, to shout, to cry … anything. Instead, almost in a trance, he rose and allowed her to guide him out of the room. Under his breath, he started to mumble a prayer.

In the kitchen, Esther was humming to herself, laying out jars across the table. The prospect of dispatching one of her captives had clearly invigorated her.

"Check the oven, Gretel," she ordered. "It must be as hot as possible for this."

Gretel looked at the ravaging flames surging inside. Then she looked at Esther – no, not Esther. The witch. She must start thinking of her as everyone else did now. Esther was nothing but a monster and the land would be better without her.

"I am not sure what you mean." Gretel's voice sounded flat and lifeless, but at least it did not wobble. *I am not afraid.* "The only things I have ever baked in this oven before are pies and gingerbread. How do I make it hotter?"

"How is it possible for you to be so slow?" grumbled Esther, and she sounded so like Ilse that Gretel sucked in a breath. The witch smacked down the jar she had been polishing and beckoned Gretel to the oven with her. Gretel complied, leaving Hansel standing limply where he was. Sweat rolled down her forehead, and she felt a little faint. Her heart beat so hard she was convinced that the witch would hear.

"Here," Esther instructed, flinging open the oven door and leaning low. "If the heat makes you wince, then it is perfect. Understand?"

"I understand," whispered Gretel. She was inches from Esther, close enough to see hair sprouting from the mole below the witch's ear and smell the bitter scent that somehow clung to her clothes, the one that put Gretel in mind of blood.

Visions fleeted through her head.

Esther, musing that all men were bullies or fools.

Esther, sharing her magic, books and knowledge.

Esther, saying how alike she and Gretel were.

She was wrong. Gretel drew a deep breath. Then, she sprang.

Esther's head snapped round. Her expression was one of sheer horror. Gretel flung herself against the witch and grabbed the key cord from around her neck, tugging until it snapped free.

But Esther had recovered. Her bony fingers clutched Gretel's arm. She was more powerful than she looked – or maybe fear was lending her strength. Gretel was forced back towards the oven.

"Help me," she yelled at Hansel. Hansel did not move. With a sudden spurt of energy, Gretel ducked away from the witch's hands – and Esther's body shot forwards, into the flames. The witch shrieked and clawed as her robe caught alight. Gretel fumbled for the oven door. Heat seared her hands. She thumped it shut. And the fire roared.

Gretel turned, panting. Her hair stuck to her face. Her hands felt on fire. The witch's shrieking died. An acrid smell permeated the air.

She looked at Hansel. His eyes were almost popping out of their sockets. Gretel's legs felt weak, but somehow she made it over to him. Her screaming hands were shaking so badly she could not loosen the ropes, and she had to find a knife to sever them. Hansel enveloped her in a huge hug. She felt him breathe into her hair.

"Oh, Gretel," he sobbed, and a moment later, fat, salty tears kissed her cheek.

NOW

GRETEL DECIDES

Two Months After the Return

When Ilse approached the manor the next day, Gretel was outside, waiting.

Ilse did not waste breath greeting her. "Have you made a decision?"

Gretel nodded.

"Is it the right one?"

"Both outcomes are right as far as you are concerned, Ilse."

"Defeat hasn't smoothed your manners, then."

The old barb stung. Why was Ilse always so unkind, so determined to make Gretel feel small? It needn't have been that way. Hurt bubbled up inside her and before Gretel knew it, she said, "Why did you always bear Hansel and I such malice? When Mother was alive, you liked us. That day we journeyed south and swam in the lake by the cornfields, and I scraped my leg. I remember you bathing and bandaging the wound because blood made Mother light-headed. You cared then. I used to look up to you."

"Life did not unfold as I wanted it to," said Ilse, in a bland voice that Gretel suspected masked anger. "Marrying your father was a mistake. But this is not about me. What is your answer?"

Gretel folded her hands in front of her, palms clammy. A gesture familiar from Westerleen and all the times she had bitten her tongue and adopted a meek silence. The thought of surrendering herself to the mercy of people who had until months ago treated her as a nobody almost broke her.

Am I going to do this?

Yes. Yes, she was.

"You have left me with little choice," she said in a low voice. "I will go to Westerleen. And there I will confess."

THEN

GRETEL'S FIRST VISIT
TO ESTHER'S COTTAGE

A Day Before the Second Abandonment

Gretel stood at the entrance to the forest, staring in between the gaps in the trees and barely breathing. Despite the frosty air, she felt hot all over. In her head, she was twelve once more, being led into the darkness by the father she had trusted. She heard the crunch of his big feet on the frosted leaves, inhaled the mossy wetness and felt the small, sharp pebbles boring into her palm.

Father had known the twins would not survive, however much he might have hoped they would.

He had left them to die. Knowingly. Walked away without a backward glance.

All because Ilse had needled him, and he didn't care enough to say no.

She gulped, battling back the memories. *I cannot let two people who so betrayed me steer the course of my life.*

By rights, she should have been at home, but Ilse was not there and everyone was distracted, still searching for the lord's missing son even though any hope that he would be discovered alive was surely in vain. He hadn't looked very hardy. Jakob had probably fallen prey to wolves or bears by now. Or Esther, of course.

Gretel almost wished she had not witnessed Brida and her friends telling fortunes a couple of days ago. The idea of seeking out the witch and discovering her fate had sunk its hooks into her and wouldn't let go. Cristoph's family agreeing to move the wedding forwards had been the final straw.

I have no time to lose. Gretel took a series of deep breaths and managed to calm her breathing. *Into the forest again.*

Cautiously, she took her first steps into the trees. Dawn was only just creeping through the canopy above her, the slivers of light just enough to guide her way. Woodsmen and hunters – those not diverted to search for Jakob – wouldn't be about for a couple of hours yet, and by then she would be deep into the forest, far from the tracks they usually walked.

As she had before, every few steps Gretel tossed a pebble on to the forest floor. They had seen her safe once before and she would have to hope they would again. She might not find the witch's cottage, of course. If it really was magic, spied only by Esther's victims, her journey would be unsuccessful.

Gretel soon fell into a rhythm. Ten steps, stone. Ten steps, stone. Avoid brambles and roots. All the time she kept alert, but the only animal she encountered was a deer which bolted the second it heard her.

No cottage appeared. Gretel began to feel despondent. This had been a foolish idea. The forest was vast. For all she knew, she could have been walking in circles the whole time. That crooked bow looked familiar, as did the holly bush beside it.

And yet… Gretel sniffed. There was a definite … sweetness in the air now. A sweetness that reminded her of the spice cake her mother used to make. Oh, how Gretel had loved that cake! Her mouth watered as she remembered the soft crumble as Mother cut it into slices, and the dense, oozing honey sweetness dancing across her tongue…

The scent was stronger now. Unmistakable. A mist trickled around her ankles and grew, cloaking the branches and leaves until Gretel could barely see in front of her. She wheeled around. The path behind her was impassive. The sweetness was thick and choking.

And there it was. Esther's cottage, looking just like a gingerbread house…

This isn't right, this isn't normal, she thought. And yet she did not run. Gathering courage, Gretel walked around the house. In the earth were bones. Boys' bones. She turned to run – then gasped, because there, just steps away, was Esther.

Gretel started. How had the witch moved so silently? Gretel found her voice.

"I… Good morning."

Esther's grin widened. "Good morning."

She doesn't appear hostile, thought Gretel. She clasped her hands, trying to project a polite deference.

"My name is Gretel. I've come because I know you tell fortunes. I would like you to tell mine. Please."

Esther threw back her head and laughed. The noise was loud and harsh, almost a wheeze, and Gretel flinched. It was the cackle from the witches in her mother's stories.

"Haven't you heard? I'm a witch." Esther's voice was reedy and strong at the same time; a woman who knew her own power.

"I have," said Gretel.

"And yet you came anyway? Oh, a mind of your own – very dangerous. Does anyone know you are here?"

Would it be safer to bluff, make out someone was looking for her? But something in Esther's watchful eyes made Gretel shake her head.

"I'm not afraid," she added, not knowing quite why she said it.

"I would be if I were you," said Esther. She turned and shuffled away. "You'd best come in."

NOW

GRETEL'S CONFESSION

Two Months After the Return

The carriage mounted the hill and began the ascent into Westerleen. Gretel kept her eyes ahead. With every passing hour, she felt sicker and sicker. Her nausea was not helped by Ilse, who was barely able to contain her smirk. Jakob sat beside her. He had insisted on coming and Gretel could not object. There was no point – he would know everything soon enough.

The carriage came to a halt by The Green Gate. Unlike

yesterday, there wasn't a crowd. People would probably have assumed she was returning to enjoy another day of the festival.

I am stone, thought Gretel, and searched for the inner hardness she had often drawn upon when she had been at her unhappiest. All she found was dread, tightening its grip on her.

The guard opened the carriage door and stood, expectant. Gretel dragged herself outside. The Westerleen man who was seeing to the horses gave her a smile.

"Back again?"

Gretel went past him and into the inn. Ilse left to fetch the villagers, who would be gathered in the meadow. At least this would be over quickly.

Jakob caught up with her as she reached the bar area. "Are you going to tell me what is going on now?"

Gretel shook her head. "If it were my decision, you would not be here."

A few minutes later, Gretel's audience started trickling into the room. Ilse had clearly wasted no time in herding up Albrect and the other men. Their expressions were wary, and a few looked disgruntled, muttering about missing the festival. With them were Gretel's father and Hansel. Father would not make eye contact but Hansel came straight over. He wore a stricken expression.

"It's Ilse, isn't it?" he said. "She kept asking me questions about you and Esther and the cottage. Kept saying, 'you don't know what you know'. If I've somehow made trouble for you, I'm sorry."

"It doesn't matter," said Gretel dully.

"Gretel," Albrect came to greet her. "What is this about? Ilse claims you have something you wish to tell us."

Gretel ran her finger over one of the scars from the oven. Seeking a fortune teller had been innocent enough. What had happened next, though...

That she did regret.

Jakob was seated, drumming his fingers along the tabletop. The ale the innkeeper had offered him sat untouched.

Gretel cleared her throat. She could not delay any longer, could she?

"I am not here because I wanted to come," she announced. "I was forced to. Ilse knows." Her stepmother scowled, and Gretel felt a surge of satisfaction. *I am not about to let you get away completely without blame. Any of you.* "What you believe is true. I did kill Esther. Therefore, I deserved the congratulations you gave me once you realized Hansel was not your saviour. No one can take that away from me."

"Gretel," Ilse's voice was warning.

Gretel ignored her. She had needed to say that, for her own pride. "Don't worry, Ilse. I am telling the truth, as you instructed. And the truth is that while you know the ending of this story, you do not yet know the beginning."

The faces watching her look baffled. Jakob's dark eyes were on her.

Gretel drew breath. "When Hansel and I were captured, it was not the first time I had met Esther, nor the first time I entered her cottage. The day before, I sought the witch out."

Hansel made a stuttering noise. "What?"

Gretel adjusted the collar of her dress. It had been a mistake to stand this close to the fire. "Let me explain…"

THEN

GRETEL'S FIRST VISIT
TO ESTHER'S COTTAGE

A Day Before the Second Abandonment

Gretel fell into step behind the witch. Her mind whirled. She was foolish. Impulsive. She might never leave this place alive. Why had she not brought a weapon?

And yet she allowed her feet to take her inside, through the sloped front door and across creaking floorboards and into a kitchen that was like nothing Gretel had ever seen, not even in her wildest imagination. Food was everywhere – there were pots on the stove, loaves cooling on the table, baskets of vegetables on the floor, dead rabbits and pheasants hanging from a rack on the ceiling. Rows upon rows of shelves were crammed with earthenware pots, pans, dried flowers and hundreds of empty glass bottles. Heat pounded from the enormous oven that covered the entirety of one wall.

An obscene size for one old woman, thought Gretel. Her fingers began to tingle as they warmed up. Perhaps it *was* true: the witch did eat people. You could shove someone into an oven like that and cook them alive…

Esther felt around for the stiff-backed chair at one end of the table and eased herself down into it, pushing aside a stack of earthenware bowls. One dipped over the edge and shattered. Esther ignored it, grabbing a lit candle. She gestured for Gretel to sit opposite.

"Well, look at you," she remarked. "Almost good enough to eat."

Gretel stiffened. Esther sighed.

"My little joke. Don't worry, I shan't eat you … unless I change my mind. And I might. Who knows?"

Tentatively, Gretel drew up the stool and folded her arms over the table. It felt sticky, as though cooking grease had seeped into it. The rest of the kitchen was even filthier. Esther leaned forwards, peering at her.

"Come closer to the candle. How old are you, girl? Twelve?"

Could the witch not see properly? "Fifteen."

"Huh. Tricky age. I assume you find yourself in a precarious situation, fifteen-year-old Gretel, otherwise you would not have risked coming to see me. Or have you run away from home? Been abandoned in the forest, perhaps? That was quite the fashion once."

Gretel glanced away.

"There are two kinds of people who have their fortune told, Gretel. One is afraid and seeks reassurance. The other needs to make a decision and seeks guidance. Which are you? Both, perhaps? Give me your hand."

Gretel stared at Esther's nails. She had never seen nails as long or crooked or yellowed. Thick lines of dirt were caked round the cuticles, and underneath. Slowly, she extended her arms across the table. Esther grabbed both hands, nails digging in.

"Let's make a deal, Gretel. I do not see why I should tell your fortune without taking something in return. Fair is fair."

"What do you want?"

"What do you think I want?"

Horrible images piled into Gretel's head. Bones and limbs,

roasting in the oven, the reek of burning flesh sweaty in the air. Blood, pooling on the cobbled floor. The door closing on her, for ever.

"I couldn't guess," she said tightly.

"I think you could. But no matter. Not saying everything in your head is no bad trait." Esther's nails dug deeper. Gretel bit back a cry. "You will clean this kitchen. You can clean, I assume? You have the hands of someone used to hard work."

"You want me to clean?" Gretel could not hide her surprise. Esther tutted.

"There you go, sounding half-witted again. You thought I wanted a nibble on your leg, didn't you? Sink my teeth into a nice juicy thigh, perhaps?"

"That is not something to joke about," whispered Gretel. "There are bones outside – I saw them."

Esther snorted. "That's right. I slaughtered a lamb last week. Or did you think those bones belonged to some other sort of creature?"

Gretel said nothing. Then, "You really just want me to clean? And then you'll tell my fortune?"

"That's right." Esther's tone was breezy. "Do we have an agreement?"

It seemed a fair exchange. Gretel wasn't sure she could trust a witch, but so far, Esther did not seem especially fearsome. "We do."

"Do not even think about leaving without holding up your side of the bargain. People are not afraid of me for nothing. Now." Esther closed her eyes. The only sound was crackling from the oven. The witch began to circle her thumbs across Gretel's palms.

"A poor girl's lot, yes…" she murmured, then went so still and silent Gretel wondered if she had fallen into a trance. Gretel was on the brink of asking if she was all right when Esther's eyelids flew open. Her voice was suddenly not the creaking witch's one, but smooth as honey.

"Your greatest fears will come to pass, every single one of them. All that awaits you is misery. You will never leave Westerleen. I see a man you do not care for, who will be bound to you for ever. A disappointed woman, whose bitterness drives her to cruelty. A boy, who will enjoy everything you crave. Any joy is fleeting. Hardship beckons – unless you can fight your fate. But then you will lose something even more valuable."

All the air left Gretel's lungs. *I knew it.* Cristoph, Ilse and Hansel – and misery. She waited. Surely there would be more. But Esther released her hands.

"Not what you were hoping to hear?" she asked. "Or exactly what you were expecting to hear, perhaps?"

Gretel rocketed to her feet. Air. She needed air. She needed to put distance between her and this dreadful place, she needed to run and not stop...

No. With immense effort, she forced herself to gulp air, gripping the wall to steady herself. A deal was a deal. She must honour it.

How Gretel managed to find the wherewithal to clean the filthy kitchen she did not know. The whole time she slopped the mop into water and scrubbed months, perhaps even years, of caked-in dirt and blood from the surfaces, her mind was screaming.

Your greatest fears will come to pass. All that awaits you is misery.

Gretel never doubted that Esther told the truth. Whatever else she might be, the witch was a skilled fortune teller. The trance had been genuine, and they had made a fair bargain.

I cannot live the life she foretold, she thought. *I would rather be dead. People can evade fate if they fight. If only I had the weapons to do so...*

But she had no weapons. She had nothing.

NOW

THE CONFESSION

Two Months After the Return

"You risked the witch's cottage to have a fortune told?" Several people spoke, but it was Albrect's voice Gretel heard. "That was heedless, foolish—"

"It felt as though I had little to lose. I saw Brida and her friends playing at fortunes and could not get the idea out of my head." Gretel sought Jakob. His face had drained of colour. Her stomach plummeted.

He knows.

He knew she had been in the cottage. And he knew what that meant.

Gretel drew in breath, then another. She knew once she revealed this, there would be no going back.

"The only way of challenging my fortune was something big, something life-changing. So I made an agreement with Esther." Now her voice cracked. "You have to understand, I was desperate..."

The men exchanged questioning glances.

"Please speak up, Gretel," said Albrect. "I am sure whatever you are worrying about cannot be so very bad."

Gretel paused, one long moment, willing it to last a lifetime. Then, she dragged her eyes to meet Hansel's.

"The witch offered me another deal."

THEN

GRETEL'S FIRST VISIT TO ESTHER'S COTTAGE

A Day Before the Second Abandonment

Gretel did not know how long she toiled but by the time the surfaces were clear and shining, her gown – which she had not thought to protect with an apron – was black with grease and dirt. Esther sat and watched. Her gaze, Gretel noticed, was often unfocused. When Gretel collected a broom from a store cupboard, she spotted a library. The shelves were thick with cobwebs and loaded with books that Gretel could only dream of reading. Never before had she seen so many in one place; so much knowledge waiting to be uncovered. She lingered in the doorway, staring, before Esther cleared her throat and she moved on.

Esther moved only twice, once to heave a tray from the oven – which she shielded the contents of – and the second time, to answer a rap at the door. Her visitor was a woman in breeches. Esther lifted a basket of glass jars filled with red liquid. Gretel noticed that her arms were shaking.

"Here," she said. "Let me."

Esther hesitated, and then handed Gretel the basket.

The woman then presented Esther with parchment, which she asked her to read and sign. Esther squinted at the words, holding them so close Gretel expected her to go cross-eyed. So, her eyesight was failing. No wonder the place was in such a state.

"I can't complain about you not working hard," remarked Esther hours later, as Gretel returned from emptying the last bucket of black water outside. "If you cook anywhere near as well as you clean, I am sure you will make some man a wonderful wife."

"If I am going to keep house for anyone, I want it to be for myself or for fair payment," said Gretel.

"Quite right. My little joke. Here." On the table was a plate, a generous wedge of some kind of cake resting upon it, and a glass of milk. "You have earned this – it's not drugged or poisoned, in case you were worried. Though I know how to do both."

"I wouldn't care if it was," said Gretel, taking a chair. She swallowed the rich, creamy milk, then took a mouthful of cake. The taste was so glorious that Gretel almost wept – bursting with warmth and spice and sweet, moist dried fruit. She finished the cake, pressing her finger against the crumbs. Esther cut another slice without asking. Gretel demolished it, not caring if she looked desperate. She could only dream of eating like this every day, as the witch did, sitting by the comfort of the fire.

"Your fortune," said Esther, "what do you make of it?"

Gretel wiped her mouth. "It is no less than I expected."

"The boy with the opportunities you lack. Might he be a brother?" Gretel was silent. Esther nodded. "Yes. You resent him."

"How can I not?" Gretel burst out. "Hansel has everything. If I was him, I would do so much, but Hansel… It's wasted on him. He doesn't realize how lucky he is."

"Such anger," said Esther. Her voice was no longer mocking. The expression on her face was almost … kind. "I was angry once, too. But I chose to change my destiny, learned to make my own fortune and live by my own rules." Gretel nodded. An idea was forming in her head – a desperate one. Was she brave enough to voice it?

Esther noticed her hesitation. "Say it, girl. Whatever you are thinking, I'm sure I've heard it before."

"I-I was thinking we could help each other." There, the words were out now. Gretel hurried on. "You drove a hard bargain, just now. When was this room last cleaned? Is the rest of the house caked in dirt too?"

"Are you offering to do something about it?"

Gretel could feel the blood thudding inside her. "You clearly need assistance. I pick things up easily, and I can read and write, too. That parchment, earlier – I could have read that out loud." Another pause. "I want to learn. Your library is the most wonderful thing I've ever seen. To live as you do... I would do anything for that."

Esther laughed. "Would the good folk of Westerleen approve of you saying such things?"

"I don't care. I do not want to go back. I crave knowledge. I want, no, need more... I don't know how to explain it any better."

For a moment, Gretel thought she'd gone too far. To be so raw and honest was to make herself vulnerable, and that was never wise. She half-expected the witch to laugh.

Esther didn't. She still appeared amused, but Gretel sensed she was thinking too … thinking hard. "You are proposing that you come and live here as my servant. Apprentice, even. Have I got that right?"

"It would help both of us," Gretel said. "I would work hard, I would help you, I would learn…"

The witch shook her head slowly. "No, my dear. Absolutely not. I can't trust you, you see."

Gretel bit her lip. She could feel this slipping away from her. "How can I prove that I am trustworthy, then?"

"When people make deals, they usually offer something the other person wants…"

Esther's words hung in the air. Gretel went still. She wanted to say she had nothing to bargain with, but the witch's meaning was chillingly clear.

This time the pause Gretel let develop was very long indeed.

I can't, she thought. *It isn't right.*

Yet, the years of misery awaiting her wasn't right either. She'd rather die than live that life. She couldn't endure it, she just couldn't. "I don't know what you mean," Gretel whispered.

"I think you do, Gretel," said the witch. "You have something that I would very much like." Now Esther paused. "That stupid, ungrateful brother of yours. He doesn't deserve his freedom. You do. And you did say you would do anything…"

Gretel's eyes felt hot and wet. She wiped the tears away. Breaking down wouldn't help.

"You would bring him to me," Esther's voice was soft and crooning. "Harden your heart, just for a moment. That's all. And then I could make your dreams come true."

The seconds passed. Gretel thought of her miserable fortune, and the wedding that would trap her for ever. She compared that life to the wonderful library, the promise of knowledge, the glorious cake. She could feel her heart hardening, just as the witch had said.

It would be so simple. And it was the only way. Here was freedom, right in front of her, if she could only reach out and take it.

"All right," she said, in a voice that didn't sound like her own. "I will."

NOW

THE CONFESSION

Two Months After the Return

Hansel's mouth dropped open, and stayed open. Everyone else appeared shocked into silence. Gretel shifted, braced for anger and disgust.

"You brought me there?" Hansel's voice was small in the silence. "Knowing she would kill me?"

Gretel badly wanted to look away but she forced herself to meet his eyes. He deserved that, at least. "I was desperate, Hansel. It made me foolish. I thought that Esther could give me freedom and for a moment I didn't care at what cost. I regretted it the moment I brought you to the cottage, but it was too late by then – that is the honest truth. That's why I gave you the chicken bone, to buy time. I was always going to save you."

"How could I have known that?" Her brother was on his feet, cheeks beet red. "You, a girl, against a fearsome witch? For two weeks, I feared every minute was my last! I was terrified. So was he!" Hansel jerked his head at Jakob, who was staring fixedly at his boots. "How could you be so cruel? You used us, without a care! Sacrificed me. You are as bad as Esther." His gaze was contemptuous. "Worse, even."

Gretel flinched, but knew she deserved his anger. "The reason I saved you was that I loved you. I cared about you all along, I just didn't know it. Even when I resented you most, Hansel, I swear it—"

Albrect seemed to wake up. "Be quiet, Gretel," he said. "We must discuss this amongst ourselves, make a judgment."

Gretel held up a hand and he fell silent. She would not be spoken over again. "Judge me all you like, but in turn I will judge you. Westerleen is backwards. It is your narrow-mindedness and fear that pushed Esther into the forest. Her skills would have been an asset to the village, if only you could have seen it. Instead, she became vengeful, and killed your sons. In the same way, you held me back. In other places, not far from here, women read, they learn, they work alongside men, and they do it well. Why should it not be the same here? We would all benefit. Can you truly say Westerleen is not a better place because of me? You, who have shared her gold between you? The fortune she amassed through your sons' blood? Yes, I did some awful things. Yes, Esther became a monster. Yet you are not without blame."

A moment passed. There was the clatter of a stool toppling as Ilse shot up, face white with fury.

"This is not the confession you promised."

"This is exactly as promised," Gretel felt wild now, and that made boldness course through her. "I have told the truth and I will tell one more. Ilse did not encourage Father to abandon Hansel and I in the forest. *I* was the one who persuaded Father to do so. Without him, I would never have got Hansel into the woods. I knew Ilse would get the blame. She deserved it. She has made my life a misery for years. Abandoning us the first time was her idea. Call that revenge if you like, but it was just."

Her father sank lower in his chair. Gretel was long past caring about his embarrassment. "So, that is my story," she said, more quietly. "You know all, now. Judge as you wish."

She turned on her heel and left. Her heart was racing, her face was hot, tears not far away, but for the first time perhaps ever, she felt truly free, as though she was soaring upwards like a bird, fresh air around her. They knew her secrets. And Gretel no longer cared. She did not need their approval, or their acceptance.

"Gretel!"

The footsteps that pursued her belonged to Hansel.

"Is everything you said really true?" he asked, in a tone that made him sound for a moment like the little boy Gretel had once been inseparable from.

She bowed her head. "Every word."

"You knew how afraid I was of being left in the forest. You held my hand when I had nightmares about it. Yet you took me there to die."

She was silent.

"Ever since you left, Father and I have inhabited the house barely speaking. I thought he didn't care. So that was a lie too."

"Father doesn't care, Hansel," Gretel said. "It wasn't hard to persuade him to abandon us. I don't hope for your forgiveness, Hansel—"

"Good," he said. "Because you shall never have it. But..."

Her breath caught. "But?"

"Maybe I do understand. Just a little. It was easier to ignore what a hard time you were having, because I was all right."

Gretel choked up. Hansel was being generous, and she did not deserve it. They both had each other wrong.

Hansel looked her full in the face. He looked different, she thought. Older. As though at last he had grown up. "I see you now, Gretel."

"And I you."

The door banged behind them. Ilse stood there. She shook with barely controlled anger. From inside came raised voices. The men arguing with each other, no doubt.

"I suppose you think you've been clever again," Ilse snarled. "Well, enjoy your moment, because it will be fleeting. The room is in uproar. You will never be welcome in Westerleen again. If you imagine you can jump in that carriage and breeze back to the manor house, you are mistaken. Perhaps your besotted betrothed will forgive you on the journey back, perhaps not. His father won't." She jabbed her finger at Gretel. "When Lord Fabian hears this story – which I will make sure he does – you'll be alone, with nothing, not even a roof over your head. Your plans will have backfired. Should have thought twice before putting on this performance, shouldn't you?"

Ilse paused for breath. Gretel tilted her head. Feeling curiously calm, she said, "What makes you think Lord Fabian doesn't know everything already?"

"Of course he doesn't. He would never tolerate your presence if he did."

Gretel took a step towards her stepmother, standing so close they were almost touching. It felt good. "He knows, Ilse, because after you tried to blackmail me yesterday, I told him everything."

THEN

THE NIGHT OF THE
SPRING FESTIVAL

Two Months After the Return

Gretel requested an audience with Lord Fabian the moment she and Jakob returned from their trip to Westerleen. She was not sure he would receive her at all – he had been busy all day receiving merchants and farmers, and no doubt had preparations to make for tomorrow – but, just as she was losing hope, a servant summoned her. The decision she had to make hung over her.

Truth, or lies.

His lordship looked weary as the servant ushered Gretel into his study. He sat behind his desk, which was piled high with parchments, books and letters. "Make this short," he said. "You are lucky I am making time to see you at all."

Had it really been two months since her first encounter with this man in Westerleen, when she had naively believed he would reward her? Gretel curtseyed, then said, "May I speak plainly, my lord? I do not want to be impudent, but I need to be honest."

Lord Fabian leaned forwards, eyes narrowing. "Speak."

"You would prefer it if I were not here."

"That is no secret."

"You allowed me to come because you believed Jakob would tire of our promise. Ottillie has told me how restless he can be."

"Yet here you are, still in my house."

"Your son is fond of me."

His lordship's eyes narrowed even further. "Are you fond of him? Or just good at getting what you want?"

She said, "I want to make a deal with you. If you agree, I will leave, and you may consider the promise broken."

Silence – the only sound was the crackling of the fire. Then Lord Fabian said, "State your terms."

Gretel took a deep breath. "I wish you to sponsor me to enrol at Levalliers University."

"Not possible," he said immediately.

He hasn't laughed, at least, Gretel thought. *That is something.* "Please give it thought. I know sponsoring a girl, especially one like me, goes against your principles, but it is not unheard of. You would not be upsetting the order of things. I don't think there is a requirement to make any sponsorship public."

"Why should I agree to this?"

"Because then Jakob will be free, and I'll be gone." Hardening her voice, Gretel said, "I never wanted a betrothal. I wanted a reward, and then I could have sought my fortune on my own terms. You wouldn't give it to me and, well, here we are."

She waited. Had she gone too far? Lord Fabian's lips turned downwards, and she thought he was going to order her to leave. Instead, he rose.

"You have audacity, I will give you that."

Was that good or bad? "I have no choice."

"And why is that? You are holding something back. If you wish for my cooperation, I suggest you tell me everything."

You can tell he trained in law, thought Gretel. She stared across the room at the bookcase. In her head, she weighed up how honest to be. Lord Fabian stood where he was, waiting.

Eventually, Gretel cleared her throat. Out the story came. Visiting Esther. Sacrificing Hansel. Everything that involved Jakob. No lies, just truth. Lord Fabian's face had remained immovable until she brought up what she still kept hidden from his son. At that he showed clear disgust.

"I could cast you out this very moment with nothing," he said. "You are aware of that, are you not? For all his rebelliousness, my son is honest and decent. He will never forgive you … this."

Gretel's voice wavered a little. "You do not know Jakob anywhere near as well as you believe. You disregard and belittle him, and you don't listen to his ideas. Maybe you should. And maybe you should tell him you think he's honest and decent to his face, too."

"Spoken by someone who cares." Lord Fabian only sounded mildly sarcastic, but Gretel still coloured. "Did you ever intend to admit your sorry story? Or do you only do so now because your hand has been forced?"

"I still rid the land of a monster. No one can argue I did not do that."

Jakob's father paced to the window and stood for a moment. Then he turned.

"I will come to an agreement with you, Gretel, but only because I want you out of my home and my son's affections. I will sponsor you. Discreetly. And you will need to be accepted by the university, but I will do it, and I will provide a basic stipend for your board and needs. View this as a delayed reward for slaying the witch." Gretel's breath caught in her throat. Was this an admission that he had been wrong?

"However," Lord Fabian continued. "My terms are thus: when you go to Westerleen tomorrow to confess, Jakob will accompany you. He needs to hear the story from your lips."

"No," cried Gretel. "I won't hurt him like that."

"Hurting him is the point. I do not want you to see each other ever again. He must realize he was wrong to befriend you, and to challenge me. There will be no forgiveness, no lingering fondness."

"But—"

"I will not negotiate. This is a generous deal, as you are astute enough to know."

Gretel closed her eyes.

Perhaps Lord Fabian was right, and this was for the best. The bond between her and Jakob could never endure, could it? For a peasant girl to enrol at a university was unusual enough. For a lord's son to keep her in his heart was another.

"Very well," she said.

NOW

THE CONFESSION

Two Months After the Return

Ilse's response came immediately. "No. You are bluffing, to give yourself time to think."

"Go to the manor and ask Lord Fabian yourself, then," said Gretel.

She and Ilse stared each other down. Then Ilse stalked back into the inn. The twins both flinched at the slam of the door behind her.

"She is going to go and spin lies about you," said Hansel. "She won't be able to help herself."

"Let her," said Gretel. "I don't care. If you ask me, Ilse would do better to leave Westerleen. There is a perfectly pleasant cottage in the forest lacking an owner."

A cottage that no longer sat shrouded in protective mist. Perhaps the power of Esther's charms and magic had died with her.

"I don't think anyone will ever want to live in that cottage." Hansel looked serious. "We found the bones, you know. They've been buried properly now. I think it has helped the families who lost someone to grieve. What will you do now, Gretel?"

"If I am permitted to travel in the carriage, I will depart." She hesitated. "You could come too."

Her brother went still. Gretel carried on. "Even if you don't want to go to the city, there are more forward-thinking towns out there, Hansel. Places that would offer you greater choices too."

"I don't think so, Gretel. Westerleen is my home."

"It doesn't have to be. Wouldn't you like to be free of Father and Ilse?"

Hansel was quiet. Eventually, he said, "I'll think about it."

Gretel hoped he did. Maybe they could become friends, one day. Maybe, though, they would never speak again. This was the price she must pay for the choice she had made. She glanced at the door. Why hadn't Jakob come out yet? Gretel had never known him to lack words. Perhaps he was too angry and disgusted to speak to her at all.

Gretel asked Hansel to go inside and find Jakob. She had no wish to confront the men again. Hansel reported that Jakob had left through the side door. The horses were in The Green Gate's stable, so he was still in Westerleen. The only place she could think he might have gone was the river.

Drawing up her hood and ducking round the villagers who stopped to greet her, Gretel found her way to the banks. Sure enough, Jakob was there. He glanced over his shoulder as she part-slid, part-jumped down the banks, then turned back to face the water. "You were in Esther's cottage before you led Hansel there," he said. "Does that mean what I think it must?"

Gretel's chest tightened.

THEN

GRETEL'S FIRST VISIT
TO ESTHER'S COTTAGE

A Day Before the Second Abandonment

After making the deal with Esther, Gretel decided to clean the windows as a final show of goodwill. Halfway through, the cloth she had been using split. Esther had dozed off in her rocking chair, so Gretel went hunting for a fresh one. When she clicked the latch on the cupboard to the side of the kitchen, it turned out not to be a cupboard at all but a door. A dank-smelling corridor opened up beyond, a darkened flight of stairs at one end.

Echoing up from the cellar was a voice.

Gretel went stiff. Surely this could only be the lord's son! So he had been captured. It sounded as though he was talking to himself.

She crept to the top of the stairs. It was difficult to make anything out in the gloom beyond a barred door, but the voice was clearer now. Gretel was sure it was Jakob.

A floorboard creaked. Jakob broke off.

"Hello?" he called. "Is someone there?"

His voice was hopeful. How could he know she wasn't Esther? The way she moved? Instinctively, Gretel backed into the shadows. Her heart thumped.

Should she let him out?

The obvious answer was yes. Whatever Esther did to the boys, not a single one had returned home safe. There might even be a reward.

But he was locked in. That meant she needed the key. Presumably Esther kept it either hidden or on her person. Gretel had seen no keys while cleaning.

If she tried to find the key, Esther would become suspicious. And Esther needed to trust her. Otherwise, Gretel would lose everything because some rude, arrogant boy had been stupid.

She couldn't risk that. Could she?

"Hello?" Jakob called again. His voice sounded desperate now.

She could try and save his life – or her own.

Gretel did not know how long she stood there. She told herself she owed the lord's son nothing. The only person she was obliged to fight for was herself.

And then she turned and walked away.

NOW

THE CONFESSION

Two Months After the Return

"You left me to die," said Jakob.

"I left you to die," said Gretel.

It felt strange to finally voice those words.

Jakob bit his lip. "And you knew you were leaving me to die."

"Attempting to free you would have been too dangerous. I needed Esther to trust me."

"That mattered more than a life? My life?"

She was silent.

"Was it all a lie?" he asked, and his voice cracked. "Our closeness, our similarities, everything we agree on? All the talk of being allies? More, even? Because that's how I felt. I was falling in—" He stopped himself. "I am no longer sure you have ever cared."

"Of course I cared," cried Gretel. She stepped closer but Jakob held up a hand, shaking his head. "I didn't know you then. I was in an impossible position. I made a choice – the wrong one, maybe."

She reached out. Jakob turned away.

"I cannot forgive you," he said. "Sorry. I would love to say I understand – that the ends justify the means – but I can't. Do you know how I feel?" He paused. "Used."

Gretel could feel him slipping away from her. She shook her head, so strongly her braid lifted off her back. "Jakob, listen to me. Since the cottage, we have been partners. Allies. That was genuine. Everything since, too. For you to care, and to understand – that means everything to me. And so do you. I mean that. The closer we grew, the worse I felt about what I did."

"Do you know what it was like?" he asked quietly. He was still looking away from her. "Sitting captive, expecting to die any moment? I have nightmares about it, even now, just like

Hansel has nightmares about the forest. Maybe they will never go away."

"Jakob…"

"There is nothing more to say." He kicked at a clump of earth. It flew into the river. "You may take the carriage home. I assume you will not be staying here. But do not expect me to talk to you ever again. Our promise ends here."

She had to tell him. She owed him that much. Quietly, Gretel said, "It is already over, Jakob. Why do you think your father did not object to you coming today?"

Jakob went pale. "He knows?"

"I knew if I didn't tell him, my stepmother would. He agreed to sponsor me at the university if I would leave you be."

Jakob went silent. Then he pulled his cloak straight. There was something brisk and business-like about the action. Something final.

"Well done," he said. "You played your game perfectly. Now you have your reward. I needn't have taught you chess. Seems you already know how to play."

Messy, mixed emotions surged inside Gretel as Jakob clambered up the bank. She wanted to run after him but knew better. Jakob was wrong. She hadn't played the game perfectly. She wasn't even sure that she had won when she had lost him.

The fortune had come true after all. She had fought her fate successfully – but not without bitter sacrifice. If she dwelt too long on that, she thought she might fall apart.

But Gretel did not fall apart. She fought.

She took a moment to inhale the fresh spring air. *I won't return to Westerleen again, unless Hansel needs me.* It was time to say goodbye.

Before she went, though, she checked the tree. Mother's book was there, carefully wrapped. She thought of Brida, who she might never see again. She would hear everything, soon. Brida would probably not understand her actions now, but Gretel liked to think she would in time. She was clever, too.

Well, Mother, she thought. *I have done what you wished of me. I have chased my dreams. I hope you are proud.*

Then, holding her head up high, she turned her back on the river.

EPILOGUE

Hair pinned up, and feeling both smart and bold, Gretel strode into the lecture theatre. A few students had already found places on the raised bench seating – books, scrolls and parchments arranged in front of them. Gretel took a place at a respectful distance from everyone else. Even a year after her enrolment, some of the male students were wary of her presence. The females too, if Gretel was honest. A low-born girl like her was an anomaly, and everyone knew it. Over time, Gretel hoped their attitude would thaw. She would like friends she could share more with than library books. Once solitary, company had become something she missed.

Adjusting to living in a city had been difficult. Instead of mud and trees there were buildings and towers, and it was noisy whatever the hour. Chatter, and merchants shouting, and dogs barking, and hooves, all blending together to create a buzz. And so many people! Women in coifs dragging uncooperative children across the pebbled streets, while others twirled wooden hoops and danced between carriages and carts. As well as market stalls, there were shops, proper shops, selling all kinds of things – meat and shoes and cloth and wooden carvings and toys and medicines – as well as numerous taverns and inns. There were plenty of fine bakeries, too, but Gretel could not bring herself to venture inside. Even the slightest hint of gingerbread spices turned her stomach.

Among Gretel's books before her was a letter Hansel had dictated. Gretel still liked to hear news from Westerleen. Her name evoked both pride and disgust. The villagers were still uncertain whether she was a hero or a villain.

She wrote to Hansel often and occasionally she would receive a reply. He was still working alongside their father, woodcutting. In her letters, Gretel would tell him about men here who taught children, who cared for them – but she knew that Hansel would most likely remain a woodcutter in Westerleen all his life.

Sometimes she remembered what it had been like as children, when they were always together. That small boy with his wide, trusting gaze. They would never be that close again – but perhaps understanding each other meant more.

The lecture theatre began to fill up. Gretel scanned her notes while she waited. Then a pile of books was slammed on the table next to her, causing her to jump.

"May I sit here?" someone asked. Gretel opened her mouth to say there was nothing stopping him but the other students' disapproval – but she recognized that voice. The words died.

"Jakob," she said. "I… What are you…"

"I don't believe we have met," Jakob's tone was formal, and he did not make eye contact as he sat beside her. "Jakob. Fifth son of Lord Fabian."

"Why are you pretending you don't know me?"

"It is normally good manners to introduce yourself when someone tells you their name."

Gretel shook her head, a little lost for words. "I am Gretel, as you well know. Why are you here, Jakob?"

"To study, same as you. My father wasn't too keen – correction, he was the opposite of keen – but I have a history of not doing what I am told, so here I am." He adjusted his books. "I wish to study law. Apparently, being argumentative is a skill I can put to good use there. I am certainly not here for the company."

Dare she hope? *Yes*, Gretel thought, *she could.* She raised her eyebrows. "Now who is being rude?"

"Perhaps we are alike," said Jakob, in his blandest voice. "I wouldn't know, having only just met you."

And for the first time, he looked at her. There was a tightness in his expression, as though he was working hard to contain himself, but, Gretel thought, a hint of something else too. Might that be forgiveness?

"Are you saying you wish to start again?" she asked softly.

Jakob rolled his eyes. "You are supposed to play along."

"This means you wish to know me again?"

"I am talking to you, am I not? And receiving chastising looks for it, no less." He directed a glare towards the front row of students, who were watching with expressions of faint disgust. "In a moment I will resume pretending this is our first meeting, but I will say this. I have been thinking. A lot. I am still hurt. But I keep coming back to this: I am here, and so are you. Neither of us were claimed by the witch. That is what matters most."

"What about my sacrificing Hansel?"

He sighed. "Desperation makes us do all kinds of things. Maybe that's why I went into the forest in the first place. And I saw how scared my sister was of the miserable life that once awaited her. So I think I understand."

Gretel released a long breath. It felt like a great pressure had lifted – but she could not allow herself to relax yet. "I am supposed to stay away from you. I promised your father. That was why he sponsored my studies. If he finds out we are even having this conversation…"

"I've spoken to him about you already. Don't worry, he won't withdraw his support. As for how I managed that, well. I have to have some secrets."

At that, Gretel laughed. "I remember the last time you said that," she said, and finally allowed herself to smile. "How is Ottillie? I thought of her a lot. I hope she has not been married to someone awful."

"She is betrothed, but she likes him, and he her. We managed to persuade my parents to allow her some choice. I am viewing that as a happy ending."

"That's wonderful. I'm so glad, Jakob." She paused. "Ottillie is not the only one I thought of a lot. I missed having an ally."

"Just an ally?"

"That is a very forward thing to ask a girl who you have only just met."

Now a smile twitched Jakob's mouth. The lecturer was arranging his books at the front. In a moment, they would need to be silent. Gretel dropped her voice. "I missed you. And I think you know that full well. When you said, by the river, that you were falling... If you were about to say what I think you were, then..." She hesitated. "I feel the same. That hasn't changed."

Jakob didn't react immediately. Then, his smile turned into a beam.

"Students!" barked the lecturer. "Cease your chatter."

"I wish to concentrate now," Gretel whispered. "I am so glad that you are here, but silence during lectures is one rule I do not support breaking."

Jakob mimed exaggerated disappointment and made a great show of opening his books. Gretel paused, glancing over her shoulder. Then, she took his hand and gave it a squeeze, just like she had by the river. And he squeezed hers back.

Gretel turned her attention to the lecture, attempting to project a serious demeanour and hide how much brighter the world suddenly felt.

She had the boy who understood her better than anyone. She had her studies. And she had her future – one far from the dismal

one Esther had foretold, and the magic of the gingerbread house.
One that was wide open ... and filled with opportunity.

One that had been worth fighting for.

ACKNOWLEDGEMENTS

Thank you to everyone who supported me in writing this book – your efforts weren't just good enough (see what I did there...), they were stellar. Specifically, I would like to thank:

Yasmin Morrissey for commissioning this project and loving the first chapter. My superstar agent, Lydia Silver, for first putting this opportunity to me. Ruth Bennett and Sophie Cashell for the initial plot brainstorming session, with added thanks to Ruth for nailing the title that had evaded everyone. My editor, Arub Ahmed, for all her fabulous insight and polishing, especially for how she encouraged me to draw out the book's themes. Genevieve Herr for her fantastic edits – there are fewer folded arms, dry mouths and wobbling voices thanks to her. Lauren Fortune for her editorial suggestions. Also thanks to Kathy Webb for copyediting, Julia Sanderson for proofreading, Sarah Dutton for her input, Liam Drane for the delicious front cover, Kiran Khanom for publicity, and everyone whose input is yet to come.

And, as always, thanks to my family and friends for your ongoing cheerleading – especially when it came to that week over Christmas when I was stuck and needed to let off steam!